THE STAND-IN

THE STAND-IN

Vanessa Graham

Chivers Press • G.K. Hall & Co.
Bath, Avon, England   Thorndike, Maine, USA

This Large Print edition is published by Chivers Press, England, and by G.K. Hall & Co., USA.

Published in 1995 in the U.K. by arrangement with the author.

Published in 1995 in the U.S. by arrangement with Laurence Pollinger Ltd.

U.K. Hardcover ISBN 0-7451-2693-6 (Chivers Large Print)
U.S. Softcover   ISBN 0-8161-7451-2 (Nightingale Collection Edition)

The text of this Large Print edition is unabridged.
Other aspects of the book may vary from the original edition.

Set in 16 pt. New Times Roman.

Printed in Great Britain on acid-free paper.

British Library Cataloguing in Publication Data available

Library of Congress Cataloging in Publication Data

Fraser, Anthea.
  The stand-in / Vanessa Graham.
    p.   cm.
  ISBN 0-8161-7451-2 (alk. paper : lg. print)
  1. Large type books.   I. Title.
[PR6056.R286S68   1995]   94-20477
823′.914—dc20   CIP

CHAPTER ONE

It had been a bad week. Natalie had a heavy cold, there'd been an unpleasant row with Clive, and to crown it all the hospital phoned to say her cousin had been involved in an accident.

'It was my own fault!' Sarah wailed when Natalie reached her bedside. 'My arms were full of groceries and my head down against the rain. I stepped off the kerb without looking.'

'Then you're lucky it wasn't worse,' Natalie said severely, eyeing the bandaged head and the arm in its stiff splint. It was strange to be admonishing Sarah, who was several years older and as a child had been rather bossy.

'I know, I know, but there's nothing I can do now except lie like a trussed chicken till they allow me to move. Which is what I want to talk to you about. You're still with the temp. agency, aren't you? Are you by any chance free tomorrow?'

Natalie reached for her handkerchief and trapped a sneeze. 'Yes, luckily. I finished with the printing firm today. Would you like some things bringing in?'

'My flat mate'll see to that, but I would be grateful if you could go and explain to my boss. Preferably as early as you can make it, because he'll be waiting for me.'

1

'Can't I just phone?'

Sarah started to shake her head and winced, one hand going gingerly to her bandage. 'Remind me not to do that! No, I'm afraid that won't do. When he's working he switches on the answer phone. It could be hours before he'd think of playing it back, and his temper wouldn't have improved in the meantime.'

'But surely it's a big office? Someone else could—'

'No, love, didn't I tell you? I changed my job at Christmas. I've been with Roderick McLaren for the last six months.'

'The writer, you mean?'

'The same. Believe me, he's not the easiest of employers. I'm expected to know such things as bullet velocity and how long blood takes to clot, but not to have opinions of my own. He regards a secretary as a tiresome but necessary extension of the typewriter.'

'Sounds delightful. Why do you stay with him?'

'For the money,' Sarah said succinctly. 'He pays extremely well. I warn you, he'll be livid about this.'

'But it's hardly your fault,' Natalie protested.

'I was stupid enough to step in front of a taxi, wasn't I? And to make things worse, he's been having trouble with the book and we've just reached a crucial part.'

Natalie sighed. 'All right, I'll try to plead

2

your case. What's the address?'

'Quite a plush one—Brunswick House, Regent's Park. He has the penthouse.'

'Wow! They don't come much plusher! I presume he's not married?'

Sarah flashed her a curious glance. 'Why do you say that?'

'Judging by his books he doesn't think much of women.'

'Quite right. He only brings them in to sleep with the hero!' She grinned. 'Come to think of it, he practises what he preaches! He's not married, you're right there, but he has a glamorous girlfriend who sometimes stays the night. Not that I'm supposed to know, of course.'

'What's she like?'

'I didn't take to her myself, but no doubt she suits him very well. She's there when he wants her but not under his feet all the time. I'd say he's got things pretty well organized.'

Natalie closed her handbag. 'You don't like him very much, do you?'

'Not a lot, but he can certainly write. The work's fascinating. If it wasn't for that I shouldn't have stuck it this long, hefty pay-packet or not.'

None of which, thought Natalie the next morning, did much to bolster her courage. Brunswick House was as imposing as its name. She caught a quick, unwelcome reflection of herself as she pushed through the swing-doors, puffy-eyed and pale, her hair unusually limp.

'Go straight up,' Sarah had advised. 'If you look business-like, the porter won't try to stop you.'

Natalie made purposefully for the lift and pressed the button for the penthouse. She wasn't aware of movement and the soundless opening of the doors took her by surprise. Nervously she stepped on to the thickly carpeted corridor. Only three doors opened off it. Directly opposite was the service room, to the left a glass exit leading to a fire-escape, and on the right an imposing door with a gilt knob. Swallowing her apprehension, Natalie pressed the bell.

There was a long silence. From up here the sound of the traffic was muted but through the glass of the fire-escape she could see the smoke-trail of a plane moving slowly across the sky. She was about to ring again when the box on the wall beside her crackled and a voice said crisply, 'Yes?'

'Good morning, Mr McLaren. I have a message for you from Sarah Berringer.'

'Where the devil is she? It's nearly nine-thirty.' The faint Scottish accent was emphasized by the machine.

'If you could spare a moment, I'll explain.'

The intercom snapped off and a minute later the door was jerked open and she was face to face with Roderick McLaren. As Sarah had predicted, he was not in the best of tempers.

4

His eyes, deep-set and a steely grey, flicked over her without interest.

'Well?'

Natalie moistened dry lips. 'I'm afraid Sarah's had an accident,' she began nervously. His brows drew together but he made no comment and after a moment she continued, 'She was knocked down going home from work last night.'

'Is it serious?'

'Not desperately, but—'

'When will she be back?'

Behind him a kettle started whistling shrilly. He said ungraciously, 'You'd better come in for a minute,' and turned on his heel, leaving her in the doorway. Tentatively she moved inside. The hall wasn't large, but its pale-washed walls gave an illusion of space. On the one opposite hung a large Impressionist painting. Beside it, an open door revealed a big room the far wall of which, overlooking the Park, was completely composed of windows.

Roderick McLaren appeared from a doorway to her right. 'I'm making coffee. Would you like some?'

'Thank you.' It might help smooth over the explanations and in any case she'd overslept and not had time for breakfast.

'Go through, then.' He nodded towards the open door and she went in ahead of him.

'What a lovely room!' she exclaimed, her eyes moving from the low stone fireplace to the brocade of the chairs and the exquisite Indian carpet which covered the floor in swirls of rose and cream.

His voice recalled her attention. 'Take a seat.' He nodded to the chair beside which he'd placed her coffee. She sat down hastily, and as he settled himself on the sofa opposite, turned her appraisal from the room to the man himself.

The strong face with its straight nose and firm chin were familiar from the dust-jackets of his books, but the black and white photographs had given no hint either of his height or the rich brown of his hair, which held more than a touch of red. Brows and lashes were paler, the mouth wilful and, she suspected, capable of passion. As her assessing eyes reached his, she found them on her and felt herself go hot, but if he noticed her confusion it didn't interest him.

'Well now,' he said briskly, 'how long is Miss Berringer likely to be laid up?'

'I don't know. At the moment she's being treated for concussion, but—'

'Two days, three?'

'You don't understand, Mr McLaren. She's broken her arm. It'll be several weeks before—'

'Weeks!' He glared at her as though it were her fault. 'Ye gods! What the hell am I supposed to do without a secretary all that time?'

Natalie drew a deep breath and continued

6

pointedly, 'Fortunately she's not in much pain. I gather it's only a hairline fracture, and the head wound did at least miss her eyes.'

For a moment his belligerent gaze held hers, but he was the first to look away and she felt a prick of triumph.

'I'm sorry, of course, about the accident,' he said brusquely, 'but you must see how inconvenient it is. I've been having problems with this book, and now that it's finally going well, the last thing I want is to have to break off and interview a succession of girls.'

'Well, I'm sorry and so, of course, is Sarah. She particularly asked me to come and explain in person.' She laid down her coffee cup and started to rise, but his voice stopped her.

'How is it you're not at work yourself, at ten o'clock on a Thursday morning?'

She stared at him coolly, resentful of the switch to personal interrogation. 'I'm with a temporary agency and finished my last job yesterday.'

'Perfect!' His hand slapped the arm of the sofa. 'Then you can help me out, surely? You must be used to picking things up at short notice, and it'll save me the trouble of—'

'Mr McLaren, I really—'

'I'll make it worth your while. I think you'll find I can be generous.'

'That's not the point,' she said helplessly. 'I've had an exhausting time recently and I was looking forward to a break. I asked the agency not to contact me for a while.'

He leaned forward. 'Look, Miss—er—'

'Blair.'

'I really am desperate. On top of everything, my father's ill and I have to fly up to Scotland for a few days. I was particularly anxious to get straight today, before I go. You couldn't possibly stay now, could you?' He glanced at his watch. 'I've an appointment at eleven, but it would be an enormous help it you could clear the backlog.'

She looked at him despairingly, his urgency reaching her despite her reluctance to commit herself. 'Well, I really—'

He smiled suddenly, sensing victory, and she was startled at the change in his appearance. It hadn't occurred to her that beneath his forbidding manner Roderick McLaren was an attractive man—a point Sarah had neglected to mention. Perhaps she hadn't even noticed. Without the need to plead for her services, he wouldn't have had to turn on the charm.

'Then,' he was saying smoothly, 'you'd still have almost a week's rest—for which, of course, you'd be paid—before my return from Scotland. And for my part I'd be spared the trouble of having to look for a secretary as soon as I get back.' Another of those curiously attractive smiles. 'Our mutual advantage, wouldn't you say?'

Ten minutes later, having shown her to the small office and demonstrated the working of the recorder, the man who was now her new employer excused himself and left for his appointment. Still not sure how she'd been talked into it, Natalie settled to work and by midday had transcribed everything on the cassettes. Wearily she sorted the papers into neat piles and covered the machines. Then she stood for a moment staring down from the height of seven floors at Regent's Park just across the road. She'd worked in less pleasant locations, certainly, and at least she had almost a week's paid holiday in which to recoup her strength. She'd spend some of it familiarising herself with the manuscript. Resignedly she picked it up and, pulling the door of the flat shut behind her, rang for the lift.

That evening, Natalie went to tell Sarah the news. Her cousin was sitting up in bed, and a measure of colour had returned to her plump cheeks.

'Oh, Natalie, I'm sorry!' she exclaimed when she heard what had happened. 'It never occurred to me he'd seize on you like that! Come to think of it, though, being a temp. you must have seemed like a gift from the gods.'

'He certainly pulled out all the stops to persuade me,' Natalie said ruefully between sneezes.

'Are you sure you'll be able to cope?'

'Oh, I'll cope—and at least I'll be keeping the job warm for you. Heaven knows, I owe you that much.'

The next day, at long last, summer came to London and Natalie took full advantage of it. Each morning she set out for the nearest patch of green and spent long hours lying in the sun, reading first the completed chapters of Roderick McLaren's new novel and then, curiosity aroused, a couple more from the library. Her cold cleared away, her skin tanned a rich golden brown, and the only remaining problem was the continuing silence from Clive. Though after their last stormy meeting it was probably for the best.

On the Thursday morning, as arranged, she set out once more for Regent's Park, oblivious of the turning heads as she swung past. Her clear brow and widely spaced brown eyes gave her an air of innocence which was oddly appealing, emphasizing the smallness of her face and the soft vulnerability of her mouth, and her hair, smooth and shining, bounced as she walked. In all, there was an air of wholesomeness about her, a healthy vitality which on that sunny morning was irresistible.

The change in her appearance obviously took her employer by surprise and he stared at her for a moment before, with a muttered apology, he stood aside to let her in.

'I'm sorry,' he said again in the hallway. 'You're not at all as I remembered.'

Natalie smiled. 'And you'd reverted to the black and white photo on your books!'

'You've read them, then?'

'One or two, yes.' He seemed to be waiting for something more, so she added, 'And I saw the one which was televised.'

'But you didn't care for them.'

She glanced at him quickly. 'Why should you think that?'

'One doesn't admit to reading an author's books and then make no comment, unless one hasn't enjoyed them.'

She flushed. 'They were very exciting.'

'Quite.' His tone was dry. 'Fortunately you're not required to like them, merely to present them in an acceptable form to my publishers. I presume you've read the new one as far as it goes?'

'Yes.'

He was looking at her with a faint frown and she realized that once again her reply had been inadequate. But when he spoke it seemed it was something else which was on his mind.

'You're younger than I realized,' he said abruptly, and, at her surprise, added, 'I'd assumed, I don't know why, that you were about the same age as Miss Berringer.'

'Does it matter?'

'I prefer to have rather more—mature women working for me.'

She raised her chin. 'If you remember, Mr McLaren, working for you was not my idea. If you've changed your mind—'

He held up a hand hastily. 'No, no—I'm sorry. I'm very grateful. It's just that some of the things I write about—' He broke off and to her astonishment she saw that he was embarrassed. He did not care for the idea of dictating those torrid love-scenes to a young and impressionable girl.

Suppressing a bubble of laughter, she said, 'I promise not to be corrupted!'

He looked at her sharply, unsure whether or not she was mocking him. Then, with a curt nod, he left her to sort out the cassettes he'd put ready. It was an hour before he returned.

'I usually have coffee about this time,' he said without preamble. 'If you'll come with me, I'll show you where everything is.'

The smallness of the kitchen surprised her, and she remarked on it.

'Since I only use it for breakfast, it's adequate. These are service flats, Miss Blair. There's a restaurant downstairs where I eat if I'm in the building. I could have breakfast there, too, if I chose.'

'I'd been wondering who did the housework.'

'All taken care of. I'm not reduced to wielding a duster myself. When you've finished your coffee, bring your book through and we'll start on the next chapter.'

They worked steadily for a couple of hours. The novel was set in New York and Natalie was impressed by her employer's detailed knowledge of the city. He seldom had to refer to the street map on the floor beside him. It was

12

just after twelve-thirty when three staccato notes sounded on the door-bell, followed immediately by a key in the front door.

'Hello?' called a light Scottish voice. 'Anybody home?'

'Damn!' said Roderick McLaren under his breath. 'All right, Miss Blair, I'll go.' He strode quickly out of the room, pulling the door half-shut behind him. Even so, the voices outside reached Natalie clearly.

'I'm sorry, Isabel, I'd lost track of the time.'

'I hadn't, I've been counting the minutes! God, I've missed you, my love. How's the old man?'

Guiltily, Natalie realized she hadn't made the same enquiry. She sat doodling on her pad, aware that though the conversation in the hall was not meant for her ears, her employer at least must know she could hear it.

'Not too good, I'm afraid. It would be so much easier if he were nearer, but as you know, nothing would induce him to come to London.'

'Stubborn old so-and-so! He'll see us all out, from sheer cussedness!'

'I hope you're right. Give me two minutes with my secretary and we'll go for lunch.' The door was pushed wider. Natalie turned and rose to her feet. 'Isabel, this is Miss Blair, who's helping out for a while. Miss Grant.'

The two girls nodded at each other. Isabel Grant was certainly lovely, tall and slim with a

13

mass of red-gold curls over her shapely head. Her eyes, green and slanting, met Natalie's without interest.

'About lunch,' Roderick McLaren was saying. 'There's a pleasant little buttery round the corner which serves snacks and sandwiches.'

'Thanks, I'll find it.'

'Take the key from the hall shelf, but I'd be grateful it you'd replace it when you return. I'll be back between two and half-past.'

As he turned away, Isabel Grant threaded her slender arm through his and a minute later the outer door closed behind them. Natalie wondered fleetingly if their love-making was as tempestuous as that enjoyed by the heroes of the novels she'd just read, then, ashamed of herself, banished the thought and closed her notebook. Roderick McLaren's private life was not her concern.

That evening, Sarah phoned to enquire how things had gone. She had been discharged from hospital to recuperate at home. 'Manage to keep your head above water?' she asked cheerfully.

'Just about. He doesn't really approve of me, though. I'm too young, and I wasn't enthusiastic enough about his books.'

'Sins of omission, both! Has the wooden heroine appeared yet?'

'Not in the book, but she called round in real life.'

'What did you think of her?'

'Beautiful.'

'And?'

'I'm not sure. Possessive certainly, but she's every right to be.'

'Specially when she comes upon her beloved with nubile Natalie instead of stodgy Sarah!'

Natalie laughed protestingly.

'Well, look at it from her position, love. There's me, knocking thirty and twelve stone, and you, all bright and dewy-eyed. Which would you choose for your lover's secretary?'

'Don't be silly!'

'It's obvious. Anyway, I at least am grateful for your stepping in—it's helped salve my conscience. Don't let him ride rough-shod over you, that's all.'

'Never mind about me, just take care of yourself. I'll pop over on Saturday to see how you are.'

Natalie was turning from the phone when it rang again.

'Clive here,' said his voice in her ear. 'Got over your cold?'

'Yes, thanks.'

'And your attack of the vapours?'

She said stiffly, 'If you're only phoning to—'

'I'm phoning,' he interrupted, 'to offer an olive branch. When can I see you?'

She hesitated, unwilling, after the trauma of their last meeting, to become involved with him again. Yet he was an amusing companion and despite herself, she was fond of him.

'There's a good film at the Odeon,' he added cajolingly when she didn't speak. 'How about tomorrow? Domino's at six o'clock?'

'All right,' she said, and, with a small sigh, went back to the living-room.

CHAPTER TWO

By the next day, Natalie was regretting having agreed to meet Clive and her mind was on the bitterness of their parting rather than the words her employer was dictating. Consequently she had started to take down a sentence before she realized that he was addressing her directly.

Confused, she looked up. 'I'm sorry. What did you say?'

'I was wondering how you'd feel about working late next Tuesday? I have to attend a meeting and would appreciate an informal record of what goes on.'

'I'm sure I could manage that.'

He returned to his dictation and Natalie to her reservations about the evening ahead.

And at first they seemed to be justified. The air of constraint between Clive and herself lasted until they took their seats in the cinema. He was good-looking, she conceded, with a swift sideway glance. The thick hair which fell boyishly over his forehead, the long-lashed eyes which she'd teased him were wasted on a boy—all these added up to a very personable young man. So why did she find it so hard to respond to his kisses? It was this difficulty that caused all their disagreements, which had culminated in the blazing row ten days ago.

'What's the matter with you?' he'd demanded angrily, when yet again she had withdrawn from the increasing passion of his embrace. 'It's not as though we don't know each other. We've been going out six months, and all I get is the same excuse—"No, Clive, I don't want to!" What the hell *do* you want, Natalie?'

She could hardly answer, 'Your friendship', but that was the truth. She was fond of Clive, enjoyed his company on their outings together, but when they were alone, with his excited breathing in her ear and his hot hands moving over her—she gave a shudder of distaste.

On the screen in front of them the usual love scene was in progress. Natalie was acutely aware of Clive, motionless beside her, and the fact that he had not, as he usually did, taken hold of her hand. Watching the screen, she found herself thinking back to the explicit descriptions of sex in Roderick McLaren's books, and to the lovely Isabel who thought nothing of spending the night with him. Or rather, amended Natalie with a twisted smile, probably thought a great deal of it. Perhaps Clive was right and she was the odd one out.

By the time she emerged from the cinema it seemed a long time since their pizza at the wine bar, and Clive bought fish and chips. To Natalie's relief he had reverted to his old self, joking and teasing and making her laugh. She wished he could always be like this, but the evening was coming to an end and she began to dread the inevitable embraces he would feel to be his due. He dropped the empty fish and chip papers into a waste-bin and slipped an arm round her shoulders. Instinctively she stiffened.

'Relax, I'm not going to molest you.' There was an edge to his voice and she bit her lip. It seemed things hadn't changed after all. 'Know something?' he went on, 'I'd decided to write you off after the last time.'

'And why didn't you?'

'Perhaps, after six months, I didn't like to admit defeat!' He gave a short laugh. 'No, it wasn't only that. I couldn't get you out of my head. You're not like the others—and I don't just mean because you put the brakes on. That difference I could do without!' He pulled her into a doorway and turned her to face him. 'I suppose the truth is I'm still hooked on you, which, since it's pretty one-sided, is my bad luck.'

'I'm sorry,' she said.

'You do like me a little, Natalie?'

'More than a little. It's just—'

'Yes, I know, but if I play it your way you
18

might change your mind. Shall we give it another try? Please?'

'All right,' she said after a minute. He gave her a little squeeze and, his arm still round her shoulder, they resumed their walking.

'Can I see you on Tuesday?'

'Not Tuesday I'm afraid. I have to work late.'

'I thought that was the man's line!'

'You won't have heard, but my cousin was in an accident and I've taken her job till she's better.'

'Which involves working late? I'm not sure I approve! What's the boss like?'

'Not bad, when you get to know him.'

'Well, I'm tied up myself on Wednesday with a squash match. I'd better phone you.' They'd reached the flat and to her relief he seemed satisfied with a quick kiss. ''Night, Natalie. Sleep well.' He waited till she had opened the door, then went quickly back down the road.

Polly was coming out of the kitchen with a mug of cocoa. 'Hi. How did it go?'

'Very well. He was sweet.' Natalie followed her into the living-room. 'Where's Jill?'

'Gone to bed. What was the film like?'

'The usual.' Natalie paused. 'I'm fond of him, you know, Poll. If only he could always be like that.'

Polly shook her head. 'I don't think he's the right one for you, hon. You should *want* him to kiss you, not dread it.'

19

'That's what he said. Perhaps there's something wrong with me.'

'Rubbish! Just because Clive doesn't turn you on, it doesn't mean no one else will.'

When Roderick McLaren opened the door to her on Monday, Natalie was concerned to see how tired he looked. Avoiding any direct comment, she asked instead if he'd enjoyed his weekend.

'I can't say I have. Most of it was spent on the phone to Scotland.'

'Your father's no better?'

'It seems not. The devil of it is, if I keep dashing up there at the drop of a hat, he'll realize how ill he is, which won't do anyone any good.'

He looked so dispirited that she searched for some means of comfort. 'Why don't you relax for a few minutes, and I'll bring you some coffee?'

He glanced at her in surprise, then one corner of his mouth lifted in a lopsided smile. 'Are you trying to mother me, Miss Blair? I'm afraid you'll have your work cut out!'

Colour blazed across her face and she stammered, 'I only—'

'Forgive me,' he said quickly. 'It was a kind thought and yes, coffee would be welcome.'

When she returned Roderick was leaning back against the sofa, his eyes closed, and again she felt a tug of concern, remembering her own feelings when her parents died. But as she bent to put his coffee down, he said without opening his eyes, 'What do women like for their birthdays?'

'It depends on the woman,' she answered cautiously.

'Isabel Grant. You've met her. What would you suggest?'

'I really don't know. French perfume, jewellery, a black chiffon—' She broke off, realizing in horror what she'd been about to say.

'A black chiffon what, Miss Blair?' He'd opened one eye and was surveying her with interest.

'Underwear,' she substituted wildly.

'Ah!'

She escaped from the room before he could comment further. That was the last time she'd waste sympathy on him, she told herself, setting down her cup with a clatter.

Perhaps because his mind was elsewhere— whether on Isabel or his father, Natalie couldn't speculate—the work was heavy going that morning. When she returned from lunch, the pages she'd typed were lying on her desk torn in half with the word 'Sorry' scrawled across them. She sighed and dropped them into the bin. Sarah had warned her he was going through a sticky patch.

She had just settled to work when she heard Roderick's key in the lock and to her surprise he came straight to the office.

21

'You saw I scrapped that chapter? Obviously nothing's going to gel today and it'd be a waste of your time and mine to press on with it. However, since you're still in working hours, could I enlist your help in another direction? Would you help me choose a present for Isabel? I'm pretty useless at these things and I'd be glad of your advice.'

Out in the sunshine he relaxed noticeably and the formality between them of employer and secretary eased a little.

'I hope you don't mind this,' he said. 'I realize it's beyond the call of duty, but I needed to get out of the house. This business with my father is getting me down and I find it hard to concentrate on anything else.'

Their destination was Harrods, always one of Natalie's favourite places, and her enjoyment that day was heightened by the feminine attention her companion was attracting. Though casually dressed in tan shirt and cords, there was an air of easy authority about him which secured them immediate attention wherever they went. Their progress was leisurely and by the time their choice had been made—a slender silver-gilt bracelet studded with seed pearls—it was nearly four o'clock.

'Tea,' Roderick said firmly. The little tearoom was busy with shoppers seeking refreshment, but as before they were attended to at once and seated at a small corner table.

'That's better!' Natalie admitted, surreptitiously easing off her sandals.

'Yes, it's an exhausting business shopping with a woman! A man simply goes into a store, says "I'll have that", and there's an end to it.'

'Then why didn't you?' she challenged. Then, realizing to whom she was speaking, she flushed. 'I'm sorry, that sounded rude. I only meant—'

'It's a good question,' he answered calmly. 'I could have done, of course, but I felt in need of company.' He looked across at her with that charming smile which was rare enough always to take her by surprise. 'So thank you for yours. I'm much the better for it.'

'I'm glad,' she said simply, and found the menu required her attention. But when she looked up, the brooding look was back on his face and he was absent-mindedly toying with a knife.

'Does your father live alone?' she asked.

'To all intents and purposes. My mother died when I was a child. There's a housekeeper who's been with us for years and my aunt lives nearby, but he gets lonely.'

'You've no brothers or sisters?'

'No, there are just the two of us—a fact for which he's constantly taking me to task!'

She waited for him to enlarge on that, but the waitress came with the tea and the subject dropped. When she'd gone, Natalie said rallyingly, 'He must be very proud of you.'

Roderick looked up, and she was startled by the bitterness in his face. 'There, I'm afraid, you're quite wrong. He considers I'd be better employed supervising the running of our Highland estate than "frittering away my time", as he put it, here in London.'

'But—your books?'

'Writing, I'm told, is no occupation for a grown man, and as if that isn't bad enough, I've failed in my most basic duty, which is to marry and provide him with a grandson.'

So that was what he'd meant. Natalie's mind flashed to Isabel. Was it possible that, having been asked to marry Roderick, she'd refused him? It seemed unlikely.

'Sorry,' he said, breaking into her confused thoughts. 'You happened to touch on a sore point, but my father certainly isn't proud of me. On the contrary, I'm a great disappointment to him.' He drained his cup. 'Shall we go?'

Whatever companionship had been between them had vanished. When they reached the pavement, he said, 'There's no point in your trailing back to Regent's Park. I'll see you in the morning.'

She nodded and stood disconsolately looking after him as he threaded his way quickly through the crowds, the uncaring sunshine bright on his red-brown hair.

There was no mention the next morning of the evening's arrangements, and on her return from lunch Natalie decided to ask what time the meeting started and whether she should eat beforehand. She tapped on the sitting-room door and had pushed it open before realizing that Roderick was not alone—was, in fact, locked in an embrace with Isabel Grant.

In that frozen instant an indelible picture of them was branded on Natalie's mind: the strength of Roderick's jaw, the sandy lashes against his cheek, and the slim hands moving rhythmically over his neck. Silent as a shadow, Natalie turned and fled to the front door, opened it again and let it bang shut. Then she went shakily to the office. Her heart was pounding and her mouth dry, yet there was no need for such a reaction. Sarah had told her they were lovers. It was the shock of coming upon them like that, she defended herself. But there was a queer, sick little knot in her stomach that she couldn't explain.

A few minutes later there were voices in the hall. Isabel glanced into the office as she passed, then to Natalie's surprise came into the room, holding out her wrist for inspection.

'Look, Miss Blair, my birthday present! Isn't it exquisite?'

Natalie glanced briefly at Roderick behind her. 'Yes, it's lovely.'

Isabel surveyed her with disapproval. 'You don't sound too sure!' she challenged. 'Don't you like it?'

Before Natalie could reply, Roderick put in

quietly, 'Of course she does—it was she who chose it.'

Natalie held her breath, her eyes going to the girl's face. All the pleasure drained out of it, leaving it expressionless, and her eyes met and held Natalie's, cold as an arctic sea. Then she said in a light, brittle voice, 'I hadn't realized. Then I'm indebted to you.'

She turned, dismissing Natalie from the conversation. 'Enjoy your stuffy old meeting, darling, though I haven't forgiven you for holding it on my birthday.'

Roderick escorted her out of the room, apparently unaware that anything was wrong. Natalie let her breath out in a long sigh. If she'd suspected from his books that he didn't understand women, it was transparently evident now. Isabel wouldn't forgive her that moment of humiliation.

The front door closed behind her and Roderick came back to the office, picking up the pages Natalie had typed before lunch and leaning against the filing cabinet while he read them through. Beneath her lowered lids she studied him—the craggy brows over keen grey eyes, the square chin and firm mouth which Isabel had claimed so passionately minutes before. And again there was that odd, painful little tug inside her. Hastily she caught up her pad and read through the last couple of pages, but her eyes only registered the squirls and loops of shorthand and she could make no sense of them.

'About tonight,' he said, dropping the sheets back on the desk. 'The meeting's in Baker Street so it's hardly worth your going home first. We could eat in the restaurant downstairs, if that's all right?'

'Yes, I'd—been wondering about that.'

He looked up. 'Anything wrong, Miss Blair?'

'No. No, nothing.'

'I'm sorry if I was abrupt yesterday. I'm grateful for your help, and Isabel's delighted with her present, as you saw.'

Until she realized I'd chosen it, Natalie thought miserably, but she managed a smile in acknowledgment.

They worked till five o'clock as usual, then Roderick pushed back his chair. 'I'm going to shower and change,' he said. 'If you'd like to do likewise, there are towels in the second bedroom.'

'Thanks, I should.' She was hot and sticky, as much from successive bouts of embarrassment as the temperature, and fortunately, not sure she'd be able to get home before the meeting, she'd slipped hairbrush and make-up into her handbag.

Roderick was at the drinks cabinet when she returned. 'We might as well be civilized about this,' he said, turning with a smile. 'What can I offer you—gin? Sherry?'

'Sherry'd be fine, thank you.'

27

He had changed into a thin suit of clerical grey, with a paler toning silk shirt. He seemed to have the fortunate knack of dressing in whatever suited him best, whether formal or leisure wear. The cut of the suit left no doubt of its pedigree and as he handed her a glass her nostrils caught the scent of his after-shave.

'Now if you'll excuse me I must ring Edinburgh.' His mouth twitched. 'Naturally I've waited for the cheap rate!'

'I thought you mentioned the Highlands?'

'The estate, yes. That's in Sutherland, but we have a house in Edinburgh, which fortunately is where Father is at the moment.'

When he left the room, Natalie walked to the window, looking down at the people thronging the pavements and others dotted over the green grass of the Park. Were it not for this meeting, she might have been spending the evening with Clive. Without analyzing the thought, she accepted that she was quite happy with things as they were.

Roderick came back into the room. 'Another drink?'

'No, thank you. What's the news?'

He shrugged. 'He sounded bright enough, but Mrs Drummond says he had a bad night.'

'Is it his heart?'

'Basically, yes, though he won't admit it. Swears he's as strong as an ox. It's because he refuses to give in that we're all on tenterhooks.' He smiled at her. 'I imagine it'll be a long time before you have to start worrying about your parents.'

She looked down at her hands. 'I haven't any, Mr McLaren. They were killed in an air crash four years ago.'

His face clouded. 'I'd no idea. I'm so sorry. Whatever did you do?'

'I went to Sarah—Miss Berringer. She's my cousin. There was no one else.'

'I hadn't realized you were related.' He paused. 'Which reminds me, I've never even enquired after her. How's she getting on?'

'Not too badly. Her head's healing well but she'll have the splint on her arm for some weeks yet.'

'If it's any consolation, I'm ashamed of myself. I'd intended to send flowers or fruit to wish her well, but my mind's been wholly on my own affairs.'

'I don't think she expected anything.'

A smile touched his mouth. 'Possibly not, she hasn't a high opinion of me. It must have been quite a responsibility for her, having you to look after.'

He seemed fixated by her youth, Natalie thought with amusement. 'I wasn't a child, you know. I'd just started college and Sarah took me in for the holidays. I'll always be grateful to her for that. When I left college and started work, I moved into a flat with two other girls.'

He put his glass down. 'We've not started the evening on a very cheerful note! Let's improve

29

it by going down for dinner.'

Perhaps because he regretted his brusqueness of the previous day, he set out to please her. Natalie could feel herself open like a flower under the warmth of his attention and found she was searching for amusing things to tell him, for the pleasure of seeing his mouth quirk when he smiled. When he glanced at his watch, she felt a shaft of disappointment.

'The meeting starts at seven-thirty. It's only round the corner, but we'll take the car so I can run you home afterwards. No argument!' he added as she started to protest. 'I wouldn't think of your going alone at that time of night.'

It was only when they arrived at the meeting that Natalie discovered Roderick was the Chairman. A hum of voices, male and female, met them as they entered the room. She hesitated, suddenly apprehensive, but Roderick guided her firmly through the crowd, replying to various greetings as they went.

'I don't want formal Minutes,' he told her in a low voice. 'They'll be issued anyway. What I'd like is a general impression of the tone of the meeting, the reception of proposed amendments and so on. But I should like a verbatim record of my own speech, since I haven't any notes and it's useful to know afterwards what one has said!'

Slowly and laboriously they worked through the agenda. It was a literary society and though famous names were frequently mentioned, they did nothing to alleviate the boredom of the proceedings. The only point of interest was Roderick's own speech, a masterly combination of wit and information. Natalie could have wished the others equally to the point. Committee members were elected, reports made, balanced sheets studied, and she faithfully noted the points she'd been asked to watch out for. It seemed endless, but at last the meeting was declared closed and coffee and biscuits served. Roderick was surrounded by people wanting to speak to him, and Natalie stayed on the edge of the crowd sipping her coffee and trying not to look out of place. Eventually an elderly committee member came over to her and kindly stood chatting till Roderick was ready to reclaim her. By then it was after ten-thirty and she was grateful for the prospect of being driven home. It had been a long and tiring day.

'I hope you weren't too bored,' Roderick said as they turned into Marylebone Road. 'I'd hoped to introduce you to some of our authors but didn't get the chance.'

'Thank you for dinner,' she said as, under her direction, he drew up in Tavistock Mews.

'It was the least I could do. Thank *you* for giving up your evening—and don't forget to claim overtime!'

As Natalie prepared for bed, she reflected that while of course she wished Sarah a speedy recovery, she hoped it would be some time before she was fit to return to work. She had a feeling that when that time came, she would be reluctant to give up her association with Roderick McLaren.

CHAPTER THREE

The telephone had been ringing for some time before, still half-asleep, Natalie stumbled into the hall to answer it.

'Miss Blair?' Roderick's voice was crisp in her ear. 'I'm sorry to wake you, but we have an emergency on our hands.'

Natalie waved back Jill, who had appeared, yawning, in her bedroom doorway. 'What is it?'

'My father's taken a turn for the worse.' He cut short her expression of sympathy. 'I've been speaking to his doctor, who tells me that whereas he could go any time, he could equally well last for a week or more. Obviously I must be with him. Just as obviously, I can't leave my work indefinitely, particularly in view of action to be taken following last night's meeting. There are sure to be long stretches of time when there's nothing to do, while he's resting and so on, when I could be usefully employed while still on hand.' He paused and Natalie heard him draw a steadying breath. 'Would it be at all possible for you to come with me?'

Her hand tightened on the receiver as her

still-sluggish mind tried to absorb what he was saying.

'I appreciate you might not want to leave London, and of course I can't put any pressure on you. Nor can I give you any idea of how long we'd be away.'

She said instinctively, 'Of course I'll come, if it would help.'

'You're sure? It won't cause any problems?'

'None that I can see.'

He released his breath. 'It would make things a lot easier. I'm very grateful. Can you meet me at Heathrow? I'll bring the typewriter and everything else you're likely to need, if you'll take the notebook you had with you last night.'

'What—what time is it now?'

'Half past six. Can you be there by eight-thirty? We'll get the first available shuttle— Terminal One of course. I'll meet you by the newsagent in the departure hall. Bring enough clothes for a week or so, and it'll be cooler up there, remember.'

He was there before her. Natalie could see him glancing impatiently left and right, and his face cleared as he caught sight of her. He came to meet her and took charge of her case.

'We've plenty of time—the next shuttle's apparently not for an hour. I'm sorry, I woke you earlier than I needed. We can have a coffee at least. No doubt you could do with one.

'I suppose,' he continued as they sat in the

33

crowded cafeteria, 'you always wish at times like this that you could somehow put things right, make up for past shortcomings.' He smiled humourlessly. 'Such as being able to produce a ready-made wife and assure Father we're just off to Eagle's Crag to run the estate!'

It was cooler and duller than of late and the greyness of the sky as they walked to the aircraft matched their mood. As the plane took off, climbing steeply, Natalie watched London fall away beneath them, the ribbons of its motorways narrowing as they gained height. When after a few minutes she turned from the window, it was to find Roderick leaning back with his eyes closed.

She opened the book she had brought, but she couldn't concentrate on it. Roderick's head slipped gradually sideways till it was only inches from her shoulder and she put up a formless little plea on his behalf, that he wouldn't have too harrowing a time in the days ahead.

As the rhythm of the plane changed for the long descent he stirred and straightened, meeting her eye with a slightly embarrassed smile. 'Sorry, was I crowding you?'

She shook her head. 'How long will it take to get from the airport?'

'Only twenty minutes or so. Drummond will meet us with the car.' He sighed. 'I'm afraid, Miss Blair, the next few days won't be easy for either of us. Still, under the circumstances,

34

perhaps we could dispense with "Miss Blair". My Calvinist upbringing makes me over-formal, I know!' He turned to her suddenly. 'This is ridiculous—I don't even know your first name.'

'Natalie.'

'Sounds like a wee midge!' he commented, exaggerating his accent. She met his smile, realizing he was trying to relieve the tension they both felt. 'And I don't suppose the sky would fall if you called me Roderick.' He leaned forward, looking out of the window. 'There's Auld Reekie below us now. We'll be down in a few minutes.'

A Range Rover was waiting for them and its driver came forward and took the cases from Roderick.

'It's a sad day, Mr Roddy.'

'It is, Jack. What's the latest news?'

'He took a wee bit of nourishment this forenoon, seemingly.'

'We'll soon be able to judge for ourselves. This is Miss Blair, by the way.' The man touched his cap respectfully and put the cases in the boot.

Natalie could feel Roderick's apprehension deepening as his meeting with his father drew nearer. She sat looking out of the window at the long, low line of hills which kept pace with them all the way into the city, wondering nervously what lay ahead. At the western end of Princes Street they turned left, driving past squares and terraces until they turned into a crescent of handsome stone houses and the car drew to a halt.

Drummond retrieved their luggage and followed them up the steps. As they reached the top, the front door was opened by an elderly woman with red-rimmed eyes.

'Oh, Mr Roddy!'

Roderick held her for a moment and patted her shoulder, then put her gently to one side. 'Bessie, this is Miss Blair, my secretary. Mrs Drummond, Natalie—a pillar of the establishment.' It was the first time he'd used her name and the pronunciation he gave it, slightly different from that of an Englishman, gave her a little spurt of pleasure.

'Your father's resting just now,' Mrs Drummond told him as they went inside. 'No doubt you'll want to look in while I show the young lady to one of the guest rooms.'

Natalie followed her up to a small room at the front of the house and, as Bessie left her, wondered if she was supposed to wait there. She opened her case and put the few things she'd brought into the empty cupboard and drawers. As she finished, Roderick tapped on the open door.

'My father's asleep,' he said. 'No point waking him, so if you're ready we'll go down. We can make a start on the "Points Arising" from last night.'

Mr McLaren had still not woken by lunch

36

time. The dining-room, like the rest of the house, was solidly old-fashioned, with heavy mahogany furniture and a stag's head on the wall. The meal was served not by the housekeeper but by a young girl in cap and apron, who seemed to Natalie straight out of the thirties. Remembering the chauffeur who had met them, it appeared Roderick's casual reference to 'a housekeeper' who looked after his father had been an understatement.

They ate almost in silence. The clock on the mantelpiece chimed twice and Natalie suddenly thought back to the previous day. At just this time she'd returned from lunch to find Isabel in Roderick's arms. It seemed a lifetime ago.

They were finishing their meal when Mrs Drummond looked round the door. 'The master's awake now, Mr Roddy. I told him the young lady's with you, and he'd like to see her, too.'

'Very well, Bessie, we'll go straight up.'

At the open bedroom door they came to a halt. Natalie could see the old man propped against pillows, but to her relief the room seemed bright and cheerful. There were flowers beside the bed.

Roderick said, 'Wait here a minute,' and went ahead of her into the room. Mr McLaren turned at his footsteps and his gaunt face lit up. He reached out a trembling hand, which his son took.

'Ah, Roderick, this is great news! A girl with you, Bessie says—and never a hint when you were here a week past! It's the best news you could have brought me—but you know that well enough!'

Natalie held her breath as Roderick cut in sharply. 'No, Father, just a minute. I'm afraid you're mistaken, it—'

'Where is she, then?' The old man was peering round his son. 'Come away in, lassie, and let's have a look at you! Ah, she's a bonny one, Roderick, she is indeed!'

'Father, listen to me. I tell you—'

Natalie was trembling as she took the gnarled hand, looking down at the old man who examined her with such keen delight. He had a mane of silver hair, a beak of a nose and strangely hooded eyes. He looked like an old eagle, she thought. She was aware of Roderick's voice in the background, explaining, talking about his book, the work building up, but she knew quite well that his father wasn't listening.

'Aye, son, you've done well. I was so feared you'd settle for yon hussie Isabel, but you've more sense than I gave you credit for. It's been a long wait, but worth it, I'm thinking.'

He fell back against his pillows, the breath rasping in his chest, and Roderick said urgently, 'Please try to keep calm, Father. The doctor said you're not to become excited.'

'Whisht, of course I'm excited! Haven't I

38

been waiting for this day the last ten years or more? Sit down, lassie—I didn't get your name?—and tell me about yourself. When are you planning to wed?' He patted the side of the bed and Natalie slowly sat. And only then, fearfully, did she raise her eyes to meet Roderick's. For a long moment their gaze held. In his, she read panic, embarrassment, and a barely formed appeal. It was to the latter she responded though she spoke to his father.

'My name's Natalie Blair, Mr McLaren.'

'Fine, fine. Now tell me, have you named the day?'

She hesitated, aware of Roderick unmoving beside her and the excited happiness on the old man's face. She really had no choice. 'Not yet.'

'Well, it's early days for you, but my time's limited, mind, and I'll dance at your wedding if it's the last thing I do! Don't delay too long, my dear!'

Roderick said woodenly, 'I think you should rest now. I—we'll be in to see you again soon.'

'You're not away back to London?'

'No, we'll be here for some time.'

'Ah!' The old man settled himself more comfortably. 'Perhaps you're right, then. It has tired me, I'll not deny it.' He reached up and grasped his son's hand. 'Thank you, my boy, for bringing her to see me.' He looked back at Natalie. 'You're the first he's brought home, my dear, in all these years. I always knew if he came back with a girl—' his breath was

39

beginning to grate again—'she'd be—the one.'

'Relax now, Father. Do you need your tablets?'

'What do I want with tablets when you've given me the best medicine in the world? I'll just take a wee rest and be right as rain.' His eyes closed. Natalie rose to her feet and walked blindly out of the room.

'Come to the library,' Roderick said.

They went downstairs in silence. He opened the door for her and she walked inside. Her mind didn't seem to be functioning too clearly. Roderick closed the door and leaned against it.

'My God!' he said tonelessly. 'What in heaven's name do we do now?' He met her eyes. 'It never entered my mind—you must believe me. I never dreamed—'

'I know.'

'But he's right. I never have brought anyone home. I remember years ago shouting at him to stop badgering, that as soon as I'd made up my mind, I'd bring the girl to meet him.' He added appealingly, 'You can see, can't you, how it seemed from his angle?'

'He looked so happy,' she said unsteadily.

'That's the devil of it. I was trying to explain, but when he started on that *"nunc dimitis"* bit, it threw me. And by then he was so excited, I was afraid that if I *did* get through to him—'

'Yes.'

They stood still, looking at each other helplessly. 'I can't expect you to keep it up,
40

Natalie. It's too much to ask.'

'But the doctor said—'

His face twisted. 'True. He hasn't got long.'

'Then,' she said carefully, 'I don't think we've any option.' Her hands were clenched at her sides. 'Remember what you said at Heathrow? If only you could put things right, present a wife to him? It looks as though you've been given the chance, A fiancée, at any rate: the next best thing.'

He pushed himself away from the door, came slowly towards her and took hold of her hands, looking searchingly into her face. 'Are you quite sure about this?'

Her heart had started a slow, heavy thumping. 'If you are.'

'Then bless you,' he said softly and, bending down, kissed her forehead. 'Now we'd better consider the implications.' He waved her to the leather sofa and they sat down. 'We can't take the Drummonds into our confidence. Bessie's a gem but she's no actress and she might let something slip. The only other person we're likely to see apart from the doctor is my aunt, Father's younger sister. We'll have to play that by ear.'

'And the doctor?' Natalie asked, belatedly realizing the complications into which their well-meaning deception was about to lead them.

'I hardly know him. Our old doctor retired last year. It's none of his concern, anyway.' He

41

smiled at her wryly. 'So it looks as though you're saddled with me as far as Edinburgh's concerned. Still, it won't be for long.'

Natalie looked down at her clasped hands. 'It's tragic, isn't it, a strong-willed man like that reduced to such helplessness. He reminded me of an old eagle, lying there.'

'Odd you should say that; he was known as Eagle McLaren at the golf club.' He flicked her a glance. 'You made quite an impression on him, too.'

'I think he'd have been glad of anybody.'

'Except Isabel,' said Roderick dryly. 'Poor girl, he's never had a good word to say for her.'

Which, Natalie thought privately, would be why they'd been delaying their marriage. 'Since he's met her, you must have brought her home?'

'That's different. I've known Isabel most of my life. She was always in and out of the house before I moved to London.'

'And she followed you there?'

'She started work there about the same time.' He stood up. 'We'd better get down to work. Despite misunderstandings that is, after all, why you're here. You can start by typing the notes we went through this morning, while I check through the last chapter.'

It was an hour and a half later that Mrs Drummond knocked at the door. 'Mr McLaren's awake, sir. He'd like you to take your tea with him.'

Roderick looked up. He hadn't moved from the sofa and the typed pages lay untouched beside him. 'Bessie—' He stopped, glancing at Natalie.

A smile spread over the woman's face. 'Aye, Mr Roddy, your father told me. I'm so glad, sir. "Why," I said to him, "he told me she was his secretary!"'

'And what did he say to that?' Roderick asked heavily.

'He said, "Stands to reason, woman, that he wouldn't tell you before me." Anyway, sir, miss, Jack and I hope you'll be very happy.'

'Thank you.' Roderick rose swiftly to his feet. 'Natalie—'

She stood up and, with an awkward smile at Mrs Drummond, preceded him from the room. She had the impression her employer was already resenting the position in which he'd been placed. His father, however, had no such inhibitions.

'Ah, there you are! Do you know this, I'm hungry for the first time in a week! Bessie's sending up a piece of bannock. Now, my dear, let me have another look at you. When I woke just now, I wasn't sure I'd not dreamed it all!'

At the old man's request, Natalie poured the tea. She was handing him his cup and saucer when he said sharply, 'You're not wearing a ring.'

Her hand shook, almost spilling the tea. This time, she thought, Roderick could reply. After

43

a pause he said shortly, 'There hasn't been time.'

'Aye, that's what I supposed. All to the good. She must have Margaret's.'

Natalie's eyes flew to Roderick and saw his face pale. 'My mother's,' he said in explanation. Then, to his father, 'It probably won't fit.'

'I think it will, but if not it can be altered. Lassie, there's a box in the wee drawer in the dressing-table. Bring it here, will you?'

With a dry mouth she did as he told her. His fingers were stiff and he struggled a moment with the catch. Then he lifted the lid and all three stared in silence at the ring which nestled inside. It was a magnificent ruby, surrounded by a circle of diamonds.

'Well, take it then!' Dougal McLaren instructed his son. 'Try it on her finger.'

'I couldn't—really—' Natalie began desperately.

'What's the matter with you, girl? I've been keeping it all these year for Roderick's bride.' He frowned, seeing her distress. 'Don't you like it? Is that it?'

She said in a whisper, 'It's the most beautiful thing I've seen.'

'Well then,' said the old man gruffly, and thrust the box into Roderick's hands. Then he caught hold of Natalie's and held it towards his son. Roderick's face was a mask.

Natalie's voice shook. 'Roderick, perhaps

44

after all we should—'

And as though to silence her, he picked up the ring and slipped it swiftly on her finger. It fitted perfectly. They both stood staring at it until Dougal McLaren said testily from the bed, 'Well, aren't you going to kiss her, damn it? You need an awful lot of prompting!'

Roderick bent forward and brushed his lips against her cheek. The old man blew his nose and settled back against his pillows with a satisfied air.

'That's fine. Now we'll have our tea.'

The ring was like a circle of fire on Natalie's finger, burning her flesh. She and Roderick sat in silence while Dougal McLaren talked animatedly about his wife, brought very much to mind by the gift of her ring, and summer days spent on the Highland estate.

'We must take you up there, lassie, it's a grand place,' he said more than once. Natalie felt he was exerting himself too much but was powerless to stop him, and across the bed from her Roderick sat unmoving. When at last the little maid had removed the tray, Roderick rose to his feet.

'I'll put the radio on for you, Father, and you can lie quietly for a while. We don't want you to tire yourself.'

The old man's high colour had faded, and the fact that he did not demur struck Natalie as ominous. On impulse she bent down and kissed his cheek.

'We'll see you later,' she promised, 'and— thank you for the beautiful ring.' He patted her hand and did not reply.

On the landing she turned blindly in search of her room, but all the doors looked alike. Roderick had come out behind her and she said in a rush, 'Which is my room?'

'The other side of the stairs. Are you all right?'

'Oh, fine!' she choked. 'Absolutely fine!' Tears were cascading down her face and he pulled her gently against him. 'I feel so false!' she wept. 'We should never have started this.'

'No, but we're stuck with it now. The ring put the seal on it.'

Natalie was silent, realizing that the last few minutes might have far-reaching effects for Roderick. Would he, after this fiasco, be able to give the ring in due course to his real fiancée, or was it now spoiled for him? Before she could stop herself, she said, 'Does Isabel know I'm here?'

'Isabel?' He sounded surprised. 'Yes, I phoned her before leaving for the airport.'

'She didn't mind my coming with you?'

'Why should she? It's no different from working at the flat.'

Of course it wasn't. But some demon inside her made her persist. 'Will you tell her, afterwards, about this?'

'I've no idea. Does it matter?' He was losing patience with her, and rightly. It was no business of hers what he told Isabel.

She said weakly, 'I think I'd like a rest before dinner.'

'Yes, of course. I'll ask Sally to give you a knock about seven.'

But though Natalie lay on the bed, she could not sleep. Her mind was whirling with the events of the day, beginning with the phone call at six-thirty that morning. Far too much had happened to be crammed into one day; it must be bursting at the seams already, and it still wasn't over.

However, the spell alone refreshed her and she felt better able to face what the evening might bring. She selected a coral dress in silky bouclé which, since it was sleeveless, showed her tan to advantage, and as Sally knocked on the door, bent forward for a last critical look in the mirror. The brown eyes were calm and clear again, a soft vulnerability the only legacy of their recent tears. She'd do. Slipping the ruby ring on her finger, she went downstairs.

Roderick was waiting in the drawing-room, which she hadn't seen before. He came forward to greet her, tall and straight in navy trousers and a pale blue blazer. 'You look—rested,' he said, but she caught the flash of admiration and was satisfied. He poured her a sherry.

'Father's still sleeping. Bessie will tell us when he wakes. In the meantime we can relax for a while.'

She glanced down at the ring. 'In that case,

shall I—?'

'No,' he said brusquely, 'keep it on. You might as well wear it for as long as we're here.' And thereafter, presumably, it would go to Isabel.

The evening passed without any summons from upstairs. Perhaps after all the traumas of the day were over. At ten o'clock, with hardly another word having passed between them, she rose to her feet.

'I think I'll go to bed now. It's been a long day.'

He stood up instantly, no doubt relieved by her decision.

'When your father wakes, give him my—love.'

Roderick nodded, his eyes on her face. She turned and went up the stairs to her room.

This time she fell instantly to sleep and for some time the disturbance in the house didn't penetrate her dreams. Then, almost directly beneath her, the front door bell rang stridently. She sat bolt upright, eyes flying open. It was dark except for the street light shining through the uncurtained window. She reached for her clock, peering at it through sleep-blinded eyes. Three o'clock. The doorbell at that hour could only mean one thing. She slid off the bed, thrust her feet into slippers and reached for her dressing-gown. Then, wrapping it round her, she opened the door.

The light was on in the corridor outside and

48

she was aware of bustle and subdued voices. The doctor was being shown upstairs. A bedroom door closed behind him and Natalie stood at her own, shivering with apprehension. After a few minutes Mr McLaren's door opened and Roderick's voice said, 'Very well, doctor. I'll be downstairs if you want me.'

Natalie heard his descending footsteps and without pausing to think, hurried after him. The hall was deserted, an inimical air about it as though it resented this intrusion on its night-time privacy. A light showed through the half-open door of the drawing-room. Natalie ran down the hall and pushed it wide.

Roderick was standing with his back to her, staring out into the dark garden. He was wearing a short, dark blue robe, and beneath it his legs were bare.

'What's happened?' she demanded breathlessly. 'Is he—all right?' Foolish question—of course he wasn't. Roderick turned sharply and stared at her and a wave of pity flooded her at the strain in his face. 'He's worse?' she whispered. She had to know.

'Yes, he's worse.' His voice was clipped. 'He's had another attack, brought on, so the doctor said, by over-exertion. No doubt that touching little drama at teatime.'

She stared at him numbly, aware that, however unfairly, he held her to blame as much as himself.

'Go back to bed,' he said. 'There's nothing

you can do.'

'Do you think I'd sleep? Please let me stay.'

He shrugged. 'As you wish. Ironic, isn't it,' he continued after a minute, 'that by doing what we thought he wanted, we should end by killing him?' His voice cracked and, appalled, Natalie ran to him, catching hold of his arm.

'Don't think that! It made him happy, whatever happens now.'

His arm tensed under her hand and she let it drop as, registering her appearance for the first time, his eyes travelled slowly over her sleep-flushed face and the thin silk gown she was clutching round her.

'Words are little comfort now. Or are you offering something more? Well?' He caught hold of her and gave her a shake.

'I just wanted to help,' she whispered.

'Then you shall, my dear, you shall.' He jerked her towards him, forcing her to arch backwards against the iron strength of his arms. Her lips opened under the demand of his and for long minutes she clung to him, aware that in the ferocity of his embrace he was punishing her for all that had happened.

Then, overhead, a board creaked and he released her so suddenly that she stumbled, bruising her hip against a chair. She clung to it for support while Roderick strode across the room, reaching the door as the doctor called from above, 'Are you there, Mr McLaren?'

Without a backward glance he went up the

stairs and a few minutes later, still shaking, Natalie returned to her room. She had no way of knowing how the old man was faring, but her anxiety for him was momentarily submerged by more personal problems. Bruised, weak, buffeted with a host of new emotions, she dropped face down on her bed and prepared to wait for morning.

CHAPTER FOUR

Eventually she must have slept, for she came to to find Sally with a cup of tea beside her bed. Memory flooded back, and she said quickly, 'Mr McLaren?'

'He's resting, miss.'

Relief swamped her. At least he was still alive. 'He wasn't taken to hospital?'

'He refused point-blank, Mrs Drummond says. Insisted if he was going to die, it would be in his own bed. She and Mr Roderick sat with him all night. Mr Roderick went to his own room just an hour ago.' She paused. 'He said to tell you you've the morning free and he'll see you at lunch.'

Natalie saw the girl's curious eyes on her face and turned on her side to escape their scrutiny. 'Thank you, Sally.'

When the door had closed behind her, Natalie slipped out of bed and went to the mirror. No wonder Sally had stared. Her

51

mouth was bruised and there was a cut in her lower lip. That, and the information that she and Roderick were engaged, hardly tallied with the curtness of his message to her, unmistakably from employer to secretary.

Remembering the night, she started to tremble. It was galling that Roderick's swift and brutal assault had stirred her more than all Clive's hot-handed advances—and it was also unfair. Clive was at least fond of her, whereas Roderick, out of his mind with grief and guilt, had simply needed to vent his emotions on a woman—any woman—and she had been to hand.

She straightened, staring into the mirror. More than anything she wanted to run away, never to have to see Roderick again. But at this stage her departure could hasten Mr McLaren's death. The bestowing of the ring had blocked any chance of belated explanations. There was no going back.

Natalie breakfasted alone in the formal splendour of the dining-room. 'Who's with Mr McLaren now?' she asked Sally when she brought in the coffee.

'A nurse has arrived, miss. Mr Roderick arranged it.'

In that case she'd go out for a while. She had no wish to skulk in a corner of this hushed house till Roderick chose to come downstairs.

Seven minutes' brisk walking brought her to Princes Street and once there she slowed her pace, allowing herself to be drawn along with the crowd in successive waves of movement as though she had no independent will of her own. It was oddly soothing and by holding her mind in abeyance, she was able to pass the whole morning with scarcely a thought of Roderick. But when the time came to return to Ravelstone Place, a knot of apprehension tightened inside her. How would he greet her after their last dramatic encounter?

Sally opened the door to her ring. 'Mr McLaren has been asking for you, miss. His sister, Mrs Downie, is with him. Will you go straight up?'

'My dear!' A smart, pleasant-looking woman of about sixty came on to the landing and took her warmly by the hand. 'Dougal has been telling me about you. I'm so very pleased to hear the news.'

'We'll play it by ear,' Roderick had said of his aunt, but his father had forestalled them.

'I'm Elizabeth Downie,' the woman added. 'I hope you'll call me Aunt, as Roderick does.' She turned with Natalie back to the sick-room and lowered her voice. 'Once again my brother seems to have weathered the storm. I sometimes think he's indestructible.'

'Is that Natalie? Come away in till I see you, my dear.'

She went to the bed and handed him a sprig of white heather she'd bought at a street stall. 'This is for luck,' she told him.

'You're my good luck, dearie, never forget it.' But he tucked the spray into his pyjama pocket. His skin had a waxier appearance than the previous day and there was an oxygen tent beside the bed, but otherwise he seemed the same.

'How are you feeling?' Natalie asked him.

'Och, I'm right enough. All this fuss, wanting to cart me off in the middle of the night. I told them I wouldn't have it.'

'We've managed to find a trained nurse,' Elizabeth Downie said.

'A waste of money,' grumbled the old man, 'but the boy insisted. It was either that or the hospital.'

'Good afternoon, everyone.'

'Roderick, my dear!' His aunt lifted her face for his kiss, catching hold of his hand. 'My warmest congratulations! Natalie and I will be great friends.'

'Thank you,' he said briefly, and, as Elizabeth Downie obviously expected, he bent and kissed Natalie's cheek. They managed to avoid each other's eyes but she felt the colour come into her face.

'And how are you, Father?'

'Well enough, my boy. I've no need of the nurse, as I told Elizabeth. An unnecessary expense.'

'You look tired, Roderick,' Mrs Downie said. 'Did you manage to get a few hours' sleep?'

'Not a great deal. I had to look through some papers.' He paused. 'You know Natalie's also my secretary?'

'Very convenient! Is she going to keep on for a while?'

The question seemed directed to Natalie, who was unprepared for it. 'We haven't really discussed it,' she said with complete truth.

During lunch Natalie found Roderick's presence a continual embarrassment, particularly since in front of his aunt they had to appear affectionate. More than once she noticed a puzzled look in the older woman's eyes. When the meal was over, Mrs Downie paused at the door on her way back upstairs.

'Perhaps you'll come and have supper with me one evening? It will do you good to be out of the house for a while.'

'Thank you,' Roderick said. Then, making an effort, 'We'll look forward to it.'

As she left the room, he said to Natalie, 'If you're ready we'll start work.'

Difficult or not, Mrs Downie's presence had meant they were not alone. Now that safeguard was removed and her heart was thudding as he followed her to the library. She sat down and flipped open her pad, waiting for him to begin, but he was standing in the middle of the room, his hands in his pockets. The silence lengthened and still Natalie waited, counting her heartbeats, not looking at him.

'You'll gather I'm not proud of what

55

happened last night.'

The moment had come, then. Her fingers tightened on her pen but she did not look up.

'Nevertheless,' he continued as she remained silent, 'you're old enough to realize that if you go running after men in your nightgown, that kind of thing is liable to happen.'

Her head jerked back, and this time the colour in her cheeks came from anger. 'You make it sound as if I deliberately—as if—' She stammered to a halt, unable after all to defend herself.

For a moment he stood looking down at her. Then he said quietly, 'I'm sorry, that wasn't fair. I was totally to blame, and I apologize. Now perhaps we can forget about it and get down to work.'

He was scrupulously polite to her for the rest of the afternoon and gradually she relaxed. The reports of the meeting were finished and she was typing them when the phone rang.

'Answer it, will you?'

She lifted the receiver, repeating the number on the disc in front of her, and a cool voice said in her ear, 'Mr Roderick McLaren, please. Isabel Grant calling.'

Natalie moistened her lips. 'Miss Grant for you.'

Roderick came across and took the phone and as she tactfully moved to the door, waved her back to her seat.

'—all night with him,' he was saying. 'It was

56

touch and go for a while. We'd quite a tussle because the doctor was all for rushing him off to intensive care and the old man would have none of it. Stubborn as a mule, even *in extremis*. He won, naturally, with the result that we've had to arrange day and night nursing, at least for the next few days.'

There was a pause as Isabel's voice crackled over the line.

'I've really no idea, love. Indefinitely, I imagine. Unless, of course he makes a marked improvement. Even that's possible. He must have the constitution of an ox to have survived last night ... The weekend?' His eyes went to Natalie. 'I don't think it's worth it, Isabel. I'm pretty well stuck in the house, you know. If it looks like being a long job, I'll fly down for a day ... Yes, of course I am ... I know. Right, I'll give you a ring in a day or two. Bye, love.'

Since it was pointless to pretend she hadn't heard the conversation, Natalie said, 'You think it's possible your father may survive?'

'Anything's possible.'

'But if he does—'

'Yes, I've thought of that. If and when he becomes strong enough, he'll have to be told the truth.'

She looked down at the ring she was wearing. 'It seemed a kindness before not to disillusion him. Now it seems more like a trick.'

'Well, we're stuck with it, and each other, for the time being. And you'll have to be a lot more convincing than you were at lunchtime. You're supposed to be in love with me—a radiant fiancée, but it took you all your time to glance in my direction.'

'You weren't,' she said tightly, 'exactly loving yourself.'

'Then we'll have to work on it before we see my aunt again. She doesn't miss much.'

'We could always tell her the truth.'

'The lesser evil?'

She held his gaze, though her face was hot. 'If you were consistent it would help. That message you sent through Sally, which obviously puzzled her, hardly tied in with—'

'Trying to compromise you in the night watches? You haven't forgiven me, have you? I've apologized, what more do you want? Damn it all, I only kissed you. I imagine you've been kissed before?'

'I thought we were going to forget it,' she said in a low voice.

'Then do so, for God's sake.' He ran a hand over his hair. 'I'm going to see how Father is,' He left the room and after a moment, Natalie went on with her typing.

At the end of the afternoon, since Roderick hadn't reappeared, Natalie attended to her own correspondence. She wrote a brief note to Clive explaining her absence, a longer one to Sarah, and a cheque for the rent to Polly and Jill, after which she put them on the hall table to await posting. When he came downstairs,

58

Roderick flicked through them, pausing for a minute. Natalie guessed he was curious about Clive, but she volunteered nothing. It was none of his business; she wasn't really his fiancée.

The next few days passed without incident. Mr McLaren seemed to be holding his own and between Roderick and Natalie there was a wary truce. Meanwhile, Mrs Downie had confirmed her invitation to supper and on the day they were due to go, Roderick again brought up the subject of their conduct in front of her.

'Don't forget, will you, that we're supposed to be in love. My aunt's an incurable romantic and she'll expect the full hearts and flowers bit.'

'Then she shall have it,' Natalie replied imperturbably, felt his quick glance and was satisfied.

She took particular care with her appearance that evening. She had brought with her a silky, biscuit-coloured two-piece which she knew flattered her. With it she wore a simple gold bangle and, of necessity, the ruby ring. Her tan had faded since her arrival in Scotland, but arms and legs were still honey-gold and she deepened the colour of her lips with soft coral.

'Has your aunt been a widow long?' Natalie asked as they drove in the direction of Corstorphine.

'Unfortunately, yes. Her husband was drowned on holiday after only six years

59

of marriage.'

'How tragic! Are there no children?'

'No. She's a happy person, though. She's made a good life for herself, and luckily money was never a problem.' He drew up outside a small grey house with a neat garden. 'So—on with the motley. Enter hero and heroine, and since she's probably watching out for us, we'll start acting right away.' And before she realized his intention, he reached across and kissed her firmly on the mouth. 'How's that for good measures?'

His eyes, faintly mocking, were enjoying her discomfiture and she resented her quickened breathing. 'Room for improvement!' she said crisply, and climbed out of the car.

There was no knowing if Mrs Downie had witnessed the incident, but she was waiting with the door open by the time they reached it, and herself kissed both of them as they went inside.

'My dear, how lovely you look! You must be very proud of her, Roderick.'

'I can't believe my luck!'

Natalie glanced at him beneath her lashes. He would pay her back sooner or later for the comment in the car, and she resolved to be on her guard. At least it had taken the complacency off his face.

'Will you pour the drinks, Roderick, while I check in the kitchen? Sit down, Natalie dear.'

Roderick went to the table on which a

60

display of bottles and glasses was arranged. 'What can I get you, Aunt?'

'Gin and tonic, please. There's ice in the bucket.'

Roderick measured the drink and said without turning, 'Sherry for you, darling?'

It took Natalie a full minute to get her breath back. 'Yes, please.'

As he handed her the glass his eyes met hers briefly but the expression in them was unreadable.

The meal was delicious and served with flair, entirely different from good but plain dishes at Ravelstone Place. It was accompanied by wine and Natalie, who was not used to alcohol, was aware of being more relaxed than was advisable in the circumstances. Nevertheless, it enabled her to respond adequately to the tenderness with which, to his aunt's obvious approval, Roderick was treating her.

When they returned to the sitting-room he joined her on the sofa, his arm casually along the back. She was acutely aware of him, the faint aroma of his cigar, the tang of after-shave she'd noticed before.

'Coffee won't be a minute,' their hostess said as she bustled back to the kitchen. Roderick's hand dropped to Natalie's shoulder and she turned enquiringly.

'"Room for improvement", I think you said. Would you care to enlarge on that?'

She was having trouble with her breathing,

every nerve in her body responding to his nearness, but the wine gave her the Dutch courage she needed. She smiled lazily and flicked his cheek with her finger.

'Don't worry about it. I'm sure you did your best!'

She saw at once that she'd gone too far. He caught hold of her hand and there was a dangerous glint in his eyes. 'You little devil!' he said under his breath.

'Right, here we are.' Mrs Downie set down the coffee tray. 'Liqueurs, anyone?'

Roderick's eyes were still on Natalie, grey and unfathomable as water. 'Thanks, I'd like a brandy, but my fiancée's had enough. I'm having trouble with her as it is!'

His aunt laughed. 'Good for you, Natalie. He's had it all his own way long enough. Cream and sugar, dear?'

'No sugar, thank you.'

As she bent forward to take it, Roderick's hand at last fell from her shoulder and she felt a tinge of regret.

'Dougal seems to be holding his own,' Mrs Downie was saying. 'Is the doctor pleased with his progress?'

'Up to a point.' Roderick took the cup she handed him. 'He won't commit himself, though.'

'It must be inconvenient, not knowing how long you'll be up here.'

'Not really, since Natalie's with me.' He was

62

referring to his work, but his aunt put another interpretation on his words, as her next question proved.

'It won't be a long engagement, will it? You have the penthouse, so it's not as though you have to embark on house-hunting.'

When neither of them spoke, she added apologetically, 'I was thinking how much it would mean to your father, to be at the wedding.'

The blood was drumming in Natalie's ears. She drank the coffee too quickly, feeling it burn her throat. Roderick said, 'We haven't any definite plans yet,' and, with a compliment on the brandy, managed to change the subject.

But as they were leaving Mrs Downie brought it up again. 'I'd like you to accept this,' she said, handing Natalie an exquisitely cut crystal bowl. 'An engagement present, since you won't give me a wedding date! Of course you must take it—' at Natalie's stammered protest. 'Never having had a daughter, or even a niece before, it's to say how happy I am with Roderick's choice. Welcome to the family, dear.'

There were tears in Natalie's eyes as they got into the car. Roderick glanced at her but made no comment until they drew away from the kerb. '"O what a tangled web we weave", etcetera. I must say you have the knack of appealing to my relatives.'

'We can't go on with this,' she said shakily.

'They're being so kind, and all the time we're deceiving them. Have you any idea how I feel?'

'I admit it's more complicated than I'd expected. But since the original intention was to ease Father's deathbed, we can hardly turn round and say, "If you're not going to die after all, we'll stop pretending."'

'Suppose I just say I've changed my mind? They'd be disappointed, but at least they wouldn't realize they'd been tricked.'

'And you'd be spared my inept love-making.'

She darted a quick look at his set profile. 'I didn't say—'

'You most certainly did. A surprising complaint, since at our last exchange I detected a fair amount of enthusiasm, despite your conventional outrage afterwards.'

'I'm sorry your pride's hurt,' she said, rushing her defences into position, 'but you can hardly expect to appeal to everyone.'

'And the last time?'

The breath was knotting in her throat. 'You took me by surprise,' she said, and turned her head away, staring out of the window at the lighted streets. It wasn't long after eleven and there were plenty of people about. What was she doing here? she thought miserably. Oh Sarah, why didn't you look where you were going?

A thought suddenly came to her, stunning her with its impact. Suppose Sarah hadn't been

64

involved in the accident, had still been with Roderick when he was called to Scotland, would events have followed the same course? Or would she, sensible, down-to-earth Sarah, have put an end to the misunderstanding before it got out of hand?

It was a relief when the car turned into Ravelstone Place and Natalie straightened, her fingers tightening on the crystal bowl. What Roderick's thoughts had been during the long silence she had no way of knowing, which was perhaps as well.

Side by side they went up the steps and into the house. In the hall she turned to him, thrusting the bowl into his hands. 'Perhaps you'll take charge of this,' she said. The bleakness was still in his eyes and on an impulse she reached up and gently kissed his mouth, feeling him stiffen with surprise.

'I'm sorry I hurt your feelings,' she said, and ran quickly up the stairs, leaving him standing staring after her.

CHAPTER FIVE

The following morning the bowl was beside her typewriter. Natalie turned to Roderick, but before she could speak he said levelly, 'As that was given to you rather than me, you'd better keep it for as long as we're together. And if you're still thinking of leaving, I'd be grateful if you'd postpone it for a while. Father had a bad night and the doctor's with him now.'

'But he seemed to be doing so well.'

'I said Dr Bruce wouldn't commit himself. Each time he recovers from one of these attacks, it leaves his heart a little weaker.' He hesitated, not looking at her. 'Natalie, I realize this last week has been difficult for you, and that my own attitude hasn't helped, but I hope you know how grateful I am for your stepping in like this. It's meant a great deal to Father.'

'He's not—I mean, he will—?'

'I don't know.' His voice softened. 'Don't look so stricken. It's what we've been expecting, after all.'

'Yes. I'm—sorry.'

'For what?' There was an odd note in his voice. 'Being fond of him?'

'No, just—not making it any easier for you.'

A knock on the door prevented his replying. Mrs Drummond looked into the room. 'The doctor'd like a word with you, Mr Roddy.'

He was gone a long time. For a while Natalie tried to concentrate on her work but she was too anxious about the old man to settle. Eventually she pushed the machine aside and walked to the window, staring out at the sedate grey houses opposite.

She was roused from her thoughts by a murmur of voices from the hall, then the front door opened and Dr Bruce went down the steps to his car. Natalie watched him drive away. The telephone chimed briefly, indicating that one of the extensions was being used. It was some time before it pinged again, and shortly afterwards Roderick's voice said from the doorway, 'I want to speak to you. Get a jacket, will you—we'll go out for a while.'

She spun round. 'He's not—?'

'No.'

'Can't we talk here?'

He said, as he'd once said in London, 'I need to get out of the house.'

Edinburgh was thronged with summer crowds, its grey streets patterned with moving streams of colour. Natalie wanted to ask about his father, why Roderick needed to speak to her, but a glance at his face kept her silent. It was clear he was deep in thought and would not welcome an interruption until he was ready.

As they entered the Royal Mile she turned questioningly, but he offered no comment on their destination so she contented herself with looking about her. It was dark and narrow here, with ancient shops and churches hemming them in, stone stairs winding upwards, a clock tower, antique shops with mullion windows. Then, at the bottom of the hill, the road opened out at the approach of Holyrood. Roderick parked the car against the Palace wall and switched off the engine. Ahead of them lay the Queen's Park and Salisbury Crags.

'Let's walk,' he said.

They crossed the road and started up the winding path. A crowd of tourists, chattering and laughing, was coming down towards them, another group pushed past from behind.

'We can't talk here,' Roderick said irritably. 'Let's make for that rock up there. It looks more peaceful.'

Natalie glanced up the steep slope to their right.

'These shoes aren't very good for climbing.'

'You can hang on to me,' he said, and took hold of her hand. They climbed in silence till they reached the rock, where they turned to look back the way they had come. They were on the side of a valley and below them the grass fell steeply away, rising again on the far side to the crag where the ruins of St Margaret's Chapel clung perilously. A triangular wedge of loch was just visible round the corner of the hill, and behind the huddle of buildings in the distance stretched the blue waters of the Firth of Forth. The breeze was stronger here, white clouds racing over the blue arc of the sky.

'After what you said last night,' Roderick began, 'I'd decided to tell Father the truth.'

She spun to face him. 'You didn't, did you? That wasn't what caused the trouble?'

'No, I didn't. What's more, I don't see that I can now.' His hand had tightened on hers, but it was an impersonal pressure, more a bracing of himself for what was to follow. 'During the night he was delirious, and all he talked about was our wedding.' His eyes were narrowed as he stared across the far water to the hills of Fife. 'He's not a religious man, Natalie, but he was—trying to strike a bargain.'

'A bargain?' she repeated with dry mouth.

'Promising to go quietly, as it were, if he could be spared until we were married.'

'Oh, God!' she said in a whisper.

'Who's Clive Rivers?' The suddenness of the question, as well as its unexpectedness, swung her head towards him, but he wasn't looking at her.

'Clive?' she faltered, bewildered by the change of topic.

'You wrote to him last week. What is he to you?'

Her eyes widened. 'Really, Roderick, I—'

'This isn't idle curiosity, I have to know. Is he in love with you?'

'Possibly,' she said after a moment.

'And you with him?'

'No.' She resented his questioning, but she couldn't lie.

'So he has no claim on you?'

She met his eyes. 'Suppose you tell me what this is about.'

Again the tightening of his fingers, and now his grip was painful. 'I was wondering,' he said expressionlessly, 'if in due course you'd agree to divorce rather than a broken engagement.'

There was a long silence, punctuated by the

call of a curlew, a child's laugh from the slopes below. Then Natalie said carefully, 'I don't think I understand.'

'I think you do.' He dropped her hand as though surprised to find he was still holding it. 'I know I've no right to ask this, you've already done far more than I could expect. I need hardly say it would be a business arrangement, to be dissolved at the earliest opportunity. And as with all such arrangements, a financial agreement would be reached. There'd be a generous settlement.'

'Money's your answer to everything, isn't it?' Natalie said. 'Whether you want a secretary, a fiancée or a wife, the solution's the same, in varying degrees.'

He said flatly, 'What else have I to offer?'

A feeling of hopelessness swamped her, which she didn't attempt to define. 'What indeed?' she said.

'I shall have to return to London shortly. Pressures are mounting and there are things needing my attention that can't be dealt with long-distance. Once there, we'd resume our own lives. You'd return to your flat and no one need be any the wiser.'

She said—and her voice was high and clear—'How soon would you want this—mock marriage to take place?'

'It would have to be this week.'

'*This week?*'

Roderick said tiredly, 'We're not talking in

70

terms of bridal veils and St Giles' Cathedral. It—'

'But even if I agreed, could it be arranged as quickly as that? I thought you had to live in the area for—'

'I phoned my lawyer as soon as the doctor left. Because of the special circumstances, he reckons we could be married almost at once. There are different laws in Scotland,' he went on when she didn't speak. 'My lawyer could prepare a petition to the Sheriff to dispense with the normal notice of marriage. Once the Sheriff approved the petition, we could go straight to the nearest Registrar.'

Natalie said the first thing that came into her head. 'What about Isabel?' And, as he looked at her blankly, 'You asked about Clive, what about Isabel? You haven't told her of the engagement, have you?'

'There was no point.'

'And now?'

'There still isn't. Discussing it with Isabel won't alter anything.'

'But you can't just—'

He said tightly, 'Suppose you let me decide what I can and can't do. Isabel and I are free agents, and the arrangement works admirably.'

'It mightn't if you were married to someone else.'

'She'll understand.'

Natalie stared at him in exasperation. Did he

71

really believe that?

'But at the moment Isabel's reactions are irrelevant.' His mouth tightened. 'I don't flatter myself you'd do this for me, but you seem fond of Father and he certainly is of you.'

'Which makes it all right to go on deceiving him?'

'Look,' Roderick said angrily, 'I'm putting myself to considerable inconvenience on his behalf. I hardly think—'

'Inconvenience!'

'I'm sorry, that could have been better put. Natalie, however badly I'm going about this, I'm asking you to marry me.'

She looked down at the ring on her finger and it starred into a prism through her tears. 'All right,' she said.

He released his breath. 'Thank you. I'll try to make it as painless as possible.'

She daren't look up, let him see her tears. She stood twisting the ruby round her finger and, watching her, he said, 'We'll have to buy a wedding ring.'

'What about your mother's?' she asked before she could stop herself. 'You made use of her engagement ring, surely—' She stopped. He was standing like a rock, staring at her.

'I'm sorry, I shouldn't have said that.'

'It doesn't matter,' he answered wearily. 'But you'll be glad to know my mother's wedding ring was buried with her.'

'I'm sorry,' she whispered again.

'I know you're upset, Natalie. It's been a difficult morning and we've both said things we've regretted. Perhaps we should concentrate on practicalities. I'll ring Jimmie Laurie when we get back and ask him to start things moving. Is there anyone you'd like to invite? Your cousin, for instance?'

Natalie shook her head. 'It's not as though it's a proper wedding.'

'My dear girl, "proper" it most certainly is. Still, with Father so ill a quiet wedding's to be expected. Today's Wednesday; would Friday be all right?'

'I suppose so,' This conversation couldn't be real. Perhaps she was still at home and the last week an extended dream.

'Then we'll fly straight back to London.'

And he could spend their wedding night with the understanding Isabel. She said with an effort, 'Is it safe to leave your father?'

'For the moment. We can fly up when necessary. We'd better go back now and break the news.'

When they reached the old man's bedroom they found Elizabeth Downie there.

'My dears. We're meeting again sooner than I expected.'

'How's the invalid?' Roderick drew Natalie towards the bed. His father was propped against the pillows, the oxygen tent near at hand. His breathing was fast and shallow.

'Not dead yet, my boy. Not dead yet.'

Roderick's arm tightened round Natalie's shoulders. 'Just as well, because we've something to tell you. We've decided to yield to pressure and get married straight away. Then perhaps we can have some peace!'

The other two exclaimed together. The old man held up his arms and Natalie bent down, feeling the beating of the frail heart under her own, his dry lips on her cheek.

Roderick was saying evenly, 'So, Father, we'll have to find you a wheelchair, because unless you put in an appearance, the whole thing's off!'

The literal truth, thought Natalie, though the others couldn't guess it.

'Have you had time to discuss your honeymoon?' Mrs Downie enquired over lunch.

'We're not bothering with one. There's a lot of work building up, and—'

'Work! My dear boy, it can wait a while longer, while you give your bride her due! As it is you're rushing her. I know it's for Dougal's sake, bless you both, but you must play fair, Roderick. Every bride deserves a honeymoon.'

'Really,' Natalie protested with flushed cheeks, 'I don't mind. I know Roderick's worried—'

'Nonsense! Even if it's just a few days, you need a little time to yourselves.'

'Very well, dear Aunt, if you insist, a honeymoon we shall have.'

74

'Leave it to me, then, you've enough to think about. Now, Natalie, what will you wear for the ceremony?'

'I hadn't thought.' She hesitated. 'I didn't bring very much with me.'

'Darling child, we're talking about your *wedding*! You must have something *new*!' She gave an exasperated little laugh. 'I seem to be more excited than either of you! Never mind, we'll go to Princes Street tomorrow.' She laid a hand over Natalie's. 'You'll forgive me organizing you, won't you dear, but you've no one of your own.'

That afternoon, Natalie went with Roderick to the lawyers and then to a jeweller where, with as little fuss as possible, they bought the wedding ring. When they returned to Ravelstone Place it was to find a message from Mrs Downie with the name and address of a hotel near Perth. Roderick went to the library and lifted the phone. When they met minutes later at Mr McLaren's door, he said quietly, 'I've changed the booking. Luckily they had a suite available.'

She nodded, not meeting his eyes, and they went in together to see his father.

The feeling of unreality had persisted and none of the actions Natalie performed— buying the ring, choosing her wedding outfit— seemed to have any direct bearing on herself. At Elizabeth's insistence, she was to spend the night before the wedding with her. 'It's bad

75

luck for the bride and groom to meet before the service,' Elizabeth decreed.

Roderick and Natalie spent that evening with Mr McLaren. Then, when he was about to be settled for the night, Roderick drove Natalie with her suitcase to Corstorphine. Elizabeth met them at the door.

'Come away in, Roderick, and we'll drink a toast before you go.'

The sight of the pleasant sitting-room with its gleaming wood and the velvet sofa recalled for Natalie the weight of Roderick's hand on her shoulder and the glint in his eyes as she'd mocked him. Had it really been only two days ago? Time had stretched and expanded beyond belief. Impossible to accept that it was barely three weeks since, on Sarah's behalf, she'd met Roderick for the first time. And now she was about to marry him.

'A long and happy life together!' toasted Mrs Downie. They had no choice but to drink to it.

'Now,' she said when their glasses were empty, 'you've a full day ahead so I'll leave you to say goodnight.' She reached up to kiss Roderick's cheek and bustled happily out of the room.

'Poor little Natalie,' Roderick said softly. 'Are you wondering what you've let yourself in for?'

'It seems like a dream.'

'It does indeed. I never thought it would

76

come to this. Perhaps,' he added quietly, 'we should practise the wedding kiss? We can't have you shying away like a startled pony.'

She stood unmoving as he lowered his face to hers, his lips, smooth and dry, moving over her own. Then he raised his head to stare into her fluttering eyes.

'There,' he said, 'that wasn't too bad, was it? Shall we try once more, for luck?'

But there was danger in his tenderness; she might find herself clinging to him, and that would put quite a different complexion on their marriage. She said with an effort, 'I think that was enough, thank you,' and his eyes darkened as he immediately released her.

'Goodnight,' he said and went out of the room. Natalie raised her hands to her face and stood for long minutes unmoving. Then, balance restored, she went in search of her hostess.

*   *   *

The figure in white in the looking-glass could not be the self she knew. Mrs Downie reached up and set a circlet of flowers in her hair, stepping back to view the result.

'Perfect!' she announced. 'You might have stepped off a wedding cake! By the way, I've arranged for a photographer. Everything was such a rush, I knew Roderick wouldn't think of it.'

Nor, Natalie was sure, would he want such a record, but she thanked Mrs Downie and allowed herself to be escorted to the wedding car which awaited them, white streamers blinding in the sunshine.

At the registry office Roderick came to meet them, accompanied by the lawyer who was doubling as best man. Mr McLaren waited in the wheelchair, his nurse in attendance, and the Drummonds stood at a respectful distance. Roderick kissed Natalie's cheek. 'You look beautiful,' he said.

The words of the ceremony were familiar, reminiscent of the church weddings of her friends. The gold ring was slipped on her finger, the formalities were over, and Roderick, his eyes unreadable, administered the 'wedding kiss' they had practised. And that, presumably, was that. She was Natalie McLaren. She repeated the name without conviction, quite unable to indentify with it.

The photographer grouped them formally, snapped, rearranged them, snapped again. There were shots of Roderick and Natalie together, some of her alone. It was part of the confusion of the day.

The little party split, the nurse and the Drummonds returning to Ravelstone Place, the others going to Corstorphine for the wedding breakfast. Where the cake had come from at such short notice, Natalie had no idea. Dutifully she ate it, drank the champagne, smiled and chatted to Jimmie Laurie and Mr McLaren. 'You'll call me Father now, if you please,' he instructed her, and pressed an envelope into Roderick's hand. 'I've not had the opportunity to buy you a present, but no doubt you'll choose something with that.'

'And I'm afraid you'll have to wait for mine,' Mrs Downie apologized. 'It'll be here when you return from your honeymoon.'

There'd been no time to choose a going-away outfit and Natalie changed into the coral bouclé she'd worn her first evening in Edinburgh. Then they were in the car and waving goodbye to the group at the gate.

'Well done,' Roderick said quietly, 'I was proud of you.' He reached into his pocket and tossed a small packet on to her lap. 'That's for you. A wedding present.'

She tore off the wrapping paper, revealing a small white box. Inside on a long chain was a golden eagle.

'It's beautiful!' she exclaimed, lifting the chain and cradling the bird in the palm of her hand. 'But I never expected anything.'

'As you know, my mother's ring's on loan and I've no doubt you'll dispose of the gold one once all this is over. It's only right you should have something to keep, and since it's an eagle it'll remind you of Father rather than me.'

Deciding it wiser not to comment on that, Natalie murmured her thanks and fastened the chain round her neck.

The Lochavie Hotel was south-west of Perth and they took only an hour to reach it. 'You needn't feel embarrassed about the change of rooms,' Roderick assured her. 'I explained I was a light sleeper and worked late, so it was simpler to have separate ones. They're not to know we're just married.'

There was a pleasant, informal atmosphere about the hotel which Natalie liked at once. Their rooms formed a suite with a bathroom between the bedrooms, and all the windows looked over the extensive grounds.

When the porter had left them, Roderick looked at her with a smile. 'On reflection, there's not much chance of concealing the fact that we're on honeymoon. You have "bride" written all over you.'

'I don't *feel*—' she began, and stopped.

'No,' he said shortly, 'I don't suppose you do. Knock on my door when you've finished in the bathroom. I'd like a shower.'

When Roderick called for her to go to dinner, it was to the outer door that he came. He was wearing a light tan shirt and trousers and cream alpaca jacket, and Natalie thought dully that he looked very handsome. The evening was a succession of disconnected images: sherry in the bar, standing shyly among strangers; the corner table in the dining-room, with a candle imprisoned in an amber bowl. The wine glass was cold to the touch, misted with condensation. Panic-stricken, Natalie wondered how they'd fill the five days they were forced to spend together before they could escape in the blessed anonymity of London.

'There's dancing in the ballroom,' Roderick commented as they finished their meal. 'Would you like to go along for a while?'

'I'd rather go straight to my room, if you don't mind. I'm very tired.'

'Of course. We'll try it another evening.'

The lift again, rising slowly and silently, reminding her of that at Brunswick House on her first visit three timeless weeks ago. They came to a halt outside her door.

'I've ordered tea for eight-fifteen, if that's all right?'

'Fine.' Natalie felt like an actress rehearsing lines.

'Goodnight, then.'

'Goodnight, Roderick.' She turned the key in the door and went inside. Holding her mind suspended, she undressed, slipped on the blue satin nightdress and went to the bathroom. And as she brushed her teeth the tears began. Hastily she retreated to her room and, abandoning herself to them, flung herself across the bed. Her stifled sobbing masked the opening of the bathroom door, but she heard Roderick's anxious voice and sat up hastily, wiping her face with her hands like a child. He was wearing the short robe she'd seen on the memorable occasion in Edinburgh. Slowly he came into the room.

'What's wrong, Natalie?'

'Nothing, really.' Her breath was still coming in gasps, her breasts rising and falling under the filmy material of her nightdress.

He said tonelessly, 'My God, what have I done to you?'

'I'm all right. It's just that—well, it's not how I've always imagined my wedding day.'

'I didn't play fair, did I, forcing your hand because you're fond of Father? But it's done now and we'll have to make the best of it. Can I get you a drink or anything? There are some in the mini-bar over there.'

'No, thank you.'

'An asprin, then?'

'That might help me to sleep.'

He went to the bathroom and she heard the click of pills and running water as he filled a glass. He came back and handed them to her, waiting while she swallowed the tablets. 'Better?'

'I shall be, yes. Sorry about that.'

A flicker crossed his face. He bent and brushed his lips over hers. 'Goodnight then, little bride. Sleep well.'

At the bathroom door he turned and hesitated for a moment. Across the width of the room they looked at each other. Then, with a smile, he went through and closed it behind him.

Natalie drew a deep breath. So she was Mrs

Roderick McLaren, but in name only. It wasn't till she was almost asleep that she realized how precarious an agreement it was. If Roderick took it into his head to claim her, she would have little chance, and no legal right, to refuse him. She was his wife, in the eyes of the law and of the world, and only the two of them knew of the private arrangement which drew such a firm distinction between appearances and fact.

CHAPTER SIX

By the next morning Natalie's natural optimism had reasserted itself. She was after all in a luxurious hotel, and she was also on her honeymoon. Even if it had restrictions not usually imposed on honeymoons, there was no reason why she shouldn't enjoy it.

At breakfast time the dining-room, which had been romantic by candle-light, was brilliant with sunshine, a large room with a wall of windows giving on to a terrace. Roderick watched with amusement as Natalie embarked on a full cooked breakfast.

'Marriage seems to have improved your appetite,' he commented.

She flushed. 'Aren't you hungry?'

'Not particularly.'

Guiltily, Natalie remembered the reason behind this holiday, but when they phoned

Edinburgh after breakfast the news was good. Mr McLaren had slept through the night and was none the worse for the exertions of the previous day.

'Don't waste your money phoning,' he told them, 'You'll hear soon enough if there's need, so go ahead and enjoy yourselves.'

Their minds at rest, they spent the morning walking round the grounds, discovering tennis courts, a pitch and put course and a swimming pool. 'That looks tempting,' Natalie said, staring down into the clear water, 'but when I left London, the last thing I thought of packing was my swim-suit.'

'No problem. There's a boutique in the foyer with quite a selection. I must say Aunt Elizabeth has done us proud. She couldn't have improved on this place.'

'You don't mind not having gone back to London?'

'No, I'm not ready for work yet, there's been too much distraction. After all,' he added dryly, 'one doesn't get married every day.'

Lunch was served under umbrellas on the terrace and afterwards, having bought swimsuits and sun-oil from the shops in the foyer, they made their way to the pool. It was deserted. 'Siesta time.' Roderick commented. 'We'll have ours here.'

They spread their towels on the grass at one side and he stripped off shirt and slacks. Natalie eyed his fair skin dubiously. 'Won't

84

you burn?'

'Fortunately no, though I don't tan either. Still, you might rub oil on my back. No point in tempting fate.' His skin was smooth under her fingers, a few golden freckles across his shoulders. 'Thanks. Now I'll do yours.'

'It's all right, I can manage.'

But he had taken the bottle from her. 'Don't argue. Turn over.' His hands were warm and strong, massaging the oil into her back and down the length of her legs. 'You've a lovely figure, Mrs McLaren,' he remarked, screwing on the cap again. 'The less you wear, the more one appreciates it.'

No reply was possible and she didn't attempt one.

The sun and silence pressed down on her and she slept.

She woke to the sound of a baby crying. There were more people round the pool now and Roderick, propped on one elbow, was watching the antics of some boys in the water. He turned as she stirred. 'Ready for a swim?'

The coldness of the water took her breath away, but she struck out after him as he set off with strong, even strokes across the pool. At the far side he turned to watch her approach, but as she reached him, breathless from her efforts, immediately launched himself on the return journey. He might have given her time to get her breath, she thought resentfully, clinging to the side rail.

There was a soft plop behind her and she turned to see a large beach ball floating on the water and, a few yards away, the smiling face of a young man. Natalie threw it towards him and a moment later was caught up in a ring of young people patting the ball from one to another. Roderick had by now reached the far side of the pool and turned, expecting to find her in his wake, but there was no pleasure in struggling backwards and forwards across the water. Natalie went on with her game.

When next she glanced in his direction he was swimming again, and moments later hauled himself out of the pool. Natalie hesitated and the young man who'd first thrown her the ball said, 'You're with him, aren't you?'

She nodded. He glanced at her hand, then back to her face, his surprise evident. 'He's your husband?'

'Yes.'

He made no further comment but tossed the ball again, and after a few minutes during which, bombarding her, they refused to let her go, she laughingly extricated herself and went back to Roderick. He did not open his eyes as she caught up a towel and patted off the surplus moisture. She felt like a child in disgrace.

Reaching in her bag for a paperback, she rolled on to her stomach and started to read. But she was disturbingly aware of Roderick at

86

her side, and careful not to brush against his long, bare leg with her own.

Eventually he sat up. 'I've had enough sun for one day. Are you coming back?'

Something in his tone antagonized her and she answered quietly, 'Not just yet.'

'Your friends have gone, if you were hoping for another game.'

She turned to look at him and his eyes fell away. 'I want to finish this chapter,' she said.

'As you wish. I'll see you at dinner.' He slung a towel over his shoulder and walked briskly away. Natalie watched him go then, with a small sigh, returned to her book.

But there was still an hour to dinner and she'd just emerged from the bathroom when there was a knock on her door. 'Natalie? May I come in? I've something to show you.'

Pulling on her dressing-gown, she went to open it. Roderick was standing outside, a newspaper in his hand, and he brushed past her into the room. 'I went down for cigarettes and saw this lying on a table. It's today's *Scotsman*. Read it.' He thrust it into her hand and she gasped as she saw the column heading.

'*Famous novelist marries. Surprise wedding in Edinburgh. "We'd no idea," say London friends.*'

*　　*　　*

'Will it be in the London papers?'

87

'You can count on it. I wonder if we have Aunt Elizabeth to thank for this, too.'

'To be fair, she doesn't know it's a secret.'

'The penalties of fame.' he said bitterly. 'Now the world and his wife know we're married, and we can't explain because of Father.'

Natalie said with a hint of dryness, 'It's lucky you and Isabel are free agents.'

Roderick sent her a black look. 'Nevertheless she won't like this, and you can't blame her. I would have explained when I saw her, but it's galling to be pre-empted like this.' He hesitated, feeling for cigarettes. 'I don't think you realize the implications.'

'I can see it's a nuisance, but—'

'For a start, you'll have to move into Brunswick House.'

She stared at him, feeling her colour come and go.

'But I can't.'

'You'll have to. Newly married couples don't live apart. It would invalidate the whole thing, mean we'd gone through all this for nothing. And though it hadn't occurred to me, there's always the chance of Father phoning and wanting to speak to you. We'd soon run out of excuses for your absence.'

Natalie said shakily, 'I'd never have agreed if I'd realized this would happen.'

'Nor would I have asked you. God, what a mess! I'd better try Isabel now—if she'll speak to me. Do you want to phone anyone?'

She shook her head. She hadn't mentioned her employer's name to Clive and her own had appeared only once. With luck, he wouldn't notice it. As for the others, Sarah, Polly and Jill—what could she say? Better put off speaking to them for as long as possible.

When Roderick came back an hour later he was still tight-lipped.

'How did she take it?' Natalie asked.

'She was not pleased. It's my own fault, I should have told her before.' Remembering her ignored advice, Natalie wisely kept silent.

During dinner they spoke no more than the previous night. Afterwards, at Roderick's curt suggestion, they went to the television lounge and sat through an American comedy. Natalie was relieved when it was time for bed.

The next morning the weather, like her mood, was less bright. 'Not pool weather,' Roderick pronounced. 'We'll take a packed lunch and go out for the day.'

The morning was clear and grey and once they'd left the main roads they seldom saw another car. They parked for their picnic in the middle of spreading moorland. Gorse misted the ground with a sheen of gold. Had it been a true honeymoon, Natalie thought painfully, they could not have asked for more privacy.

She looked up at Roderick as he gazed out across the distance, body braced in the wind, eyes narrowed, and a wave of weakness washed over her. Why couldn't she forget the way he had held her, that first night in Edinburgh? Having so roundly condemned the loveless couplings in his books, it was ironic that she should now be longing for his touch. Yet not, after all, inconsistent.

She drew a shuddering breath and, at last admitting the truth, found it no surprise. Even at the beginning, her reaction when she'd found him with Isabel had been unacknowledged jealousy. And there were complications on his side, too. He might consider their marriage inconvenient, but she knew from the times he'd held her and the expression sometimes in his eyes that as a woman she attracted him. The strain between them was certain to increase.

His voice recalled her. 'You're looking very pensive. Come on, let's walk for a while.'

The moss was springy under her feet, the sky a grey arch studded with bird-song and Roderick's hand, warm and strong, guided her over the rough ground. It was all so perfect, except for one thing, and it didn't do to dwell on that. It was as they turned to go back to the car that her foot caught in a rabbit hole and she stumbled. He caught her instantly, the swift upward jerk of his hand spinning her against him. Flustered, she straightened, murmuring her thanks, but he didn't move and as she raised her eyes to his, what she saw there sent the blood thundering through her veins.

He said very softly, 'You know, little wife who isn't a wife, I have a problem. We're together all day long, my ring's on your finger, and I'm the envy of our fellow guests. But when bedtime comes round, we smile politely and go our separate ways. And I have to tell you this does nothing for my blood pressure.'

He was tracing the outline of her chin with one finger and she said in a rush, 'Roderick, I think—'

'Furthermore,' he went on even more softly, as he drew her closer, 'we still have that complaint to deal with. "Room for improvement", didn't you say? We can't have dissatisfied customers.'

For the space of a few seconds she allowed herself to return his kisses before, as they grew more demanding, she pushed him away. 'No!' she said breathlessly.

'Why the hell not? We're married, aren't we? It's all legal and above-board.'

Confident of his argument he was again pulling her towards him and she strained backwards. 'No, Roderick. Please.' Every word required a fresh intake of breath, a bellows-like expulsion from her lungs. 'You said—you wouldn't.'

Minutes ticked by before his hands dropped from her arms. With dulled eyes she stared down at a tiny ant manoeuvring its way over a stem of heather. She was a fool, she thought despairingly. She loved him, he wanted her, and as he said, they were married. What possible reason could she have for refusing him? But she knew the answer. Once again she heard Sarah telling her the women in his books were only there for one purpose, and 'he practises what he preaches.' It was pride alone that kept her from him.

'Look at me, Natalie.'

Slowly she raised her head, seeing him with a clarity of vision that was painful, her eyes moving inch by inch over the soft camel of his sweater, his square chin and sensuous, wilful mouth, to the sandy fringe of lashes above the intense grey eyes.

'Now,' he said unevenly, 'tell me you don't want me to make love to you.'

'I don't want you to make love to me.'

For a moment longer his eyes remained locked on hers, willing her to change her mind. Then he turned away. 'You and your body should get together,' he said curtly. 'You've got your signals crossed.'

With the need to resist him past, she sank limply on to the heather, tears filling her eyes. He was waiting for her but she couldn't move, couldn't trust the trembling vulnerability which might betray her.

'Get up,' he said finally. 'I can't leave you there. People might get the wrong impression.'

As she stumbled to her feet he made no attempt to help her. Perhaps he didn't trust himself, either. Side by side, not speaking, they made their way back to the car. Roderick's mouth was grim, his eyes like slate. He opened the car door for her and as he got in beside her, said abruptly, 'I'm not going to apologize, if that's what you're waiting for. What's more, I've no intention of saying it won't happen again. It probably will. I'm flesh and blood, after all, and you don't exactly dress like a nun.'

'Would you rather I wore black bombazine?' It was a feeble attempt at defiance and he made short work of it.

'As I thought I'd made clear, I'd rather you wore nothing at all!' He gave a brief laugh. 'I must say I'm not used to such coyness. It adds a touch of piquancy—I must use it in one of my books.'

Natalie said tightly, 'I'm glad I'm giving you copy.'

'A pity it's all you're giving me!'

She sat rigidly beside him, eyes fixed on the road. The exchange had at least confirmed there was nothing personal in his desire; it was simply a challenge to wear down her resistance. The humiliation was that he could so easily succeed.

*　　　*　　　*

After dinner that evening they started talking to an elderly couple in the lounge. Natalie was still uncomfortable in Roderick's company

93

and only too ready to encourage overtures from the other guests. The young people she'd seen in the pool were in a laughing crowd at the far end of the room and she'd have preferred to join them, but there was little chance of that.

The old couple had just returned from visiting their son in Australia, which provided a fund of conversation that lasted them throughout the evening. With only nominal prompting they set off on one long story after another, and Natalie found her attention wandering. More than once, she looked up to find her husband's eyes on her face, and at ten o'clock, unable to sit still any longer, she excused herself.

'There's no need for you to come, dear,' she added as Roderick also rose to his feet. 'It's still early—I'm just feeling rather tired.' And as he hesitated, the old gentleman embarked on another story.

Natalie walked across to the lifts and rang the bell.

'Hi!' said a cheery voice behind her, and she turned to see the boy from the pool. 'Not off to bed already, surely? We're going down to the basement for a game of table-tennis. Why not join us?'

'Oh, I couldn't. I mean—'

He grinned. 'Your husband doesn't beat you, does he? Anyway, if old Mr Barlow's collared him, he's there for the night! You'll be back before he misses you. My name's Steve, by the way. And you're—?'

'Natalie.'

'Right, come on then. The others have gone down.'

For the next couple of hours Natalie thoroughly enjoyed herself. She'd seen no one of her own age since leaving London, and she could relax with this young crowd as she couldn't with Roderick. It was after midnight when she reached her bedroom and she suppressed a slight feeling of guilt. But she hadn't done anything wrong, she told herself defiantly, and Roderick probably knew nothing about it anyway. He was unlikely to have checked up on her.

At breakfast, though, he said with studied casualness, 'Did you enjoy yourself last night?'

She looked at him quickly. 'Last night?'

'After you ditched me. Was that a chance meeting at the lift, or pre-arranged?'

Colour flooded her face. 'Pure chance,' she said stiffly. 'Does it matter?'

'Not as long as you're discreet. But when you tell your husband in front of witnesses that you're going to bed and then, in front of same witnesses, veer off in a completely different direction with another man, it could lead to complications. The lifts are visible from where we were sitting, you know.'

'I didn't realize.'

'Obviously not. So where were you, till past midnight?'

She bit her lip, resenting his questions but aware he had a right to ask them. 'Playing table-tennis,' she said unwillingly.

'Well, that's a new line, anyway.'

'It's not a line, Roderick, and we weren't alone.'

'Didn't it strike them as odd that you should abandon me for so long?'

'I don't think we thought about it. Anyway, what we do here won't get back to your father,' she added rebelliously. 'I thought that was all that worried you.'

'Father or no, I have no intention of being made to look a fool. You were careful to assure me I needn't accompany you, remember. So, to restore appearances, we'll give a display of togetherness today. I'm sorry, but you brought it on yourself. This morning you can accompany me round the pitch and put course and this afternoon we'll go to the pool, where I'll expect you to stay dutifully at my side however many games of ball are in progress.'

'Detention!' said Natalie bitterly.

His mouth tightened. 'Precisely. Unpleasant, but in the circumstances necessary to restore my *amour propre*.'

Accordingly they followed the programme he had outlined and gradually the fresh air and exercise smoothed the edges of their irritation with each other and they began to relax. Fortunately Steve and the others were not at the pool, and whatever the reason for it,

Natalie found Roderick's undivided attention very gratifying. All in all it was a better day than had seemed possible at breakfast.

As they finished dinner that evening, Roderick suggested they make their way to the ballroom. 'I've no wish to be caught by the Barlows again!' he added humorously. Music came to meet them as they went down the corridor. The ballroom was dimly lit. It felt very warm, though the long windows leading to the terrace were all open.

Roderick took off his jacket and hung it on the back of a chair. 'Come and dance,' he said. And only as his arms went round her did Natalie realize this was yet another ploy in the siege he was laying to her. Stoically she set herself to withstand it.

Fortunately for her peace of mind the selection of slow dances was just ending and for the next half-hour they danced opposite each other, touching only briefly to spin each other round. Roderick knew all the latest steps and Natalie concluded he must go to night-clubs with Isabel. Then the slow music started again and she allowed herself to be drawn into the circle of his arms. He held her tightly, his lips brushing her cheek, and she drifted with him in time to the sensuous music, her resolve to resist him disintegrating. Was this still to impress any fellow guests who might be watching them? That it was not was soon made clear.

97

'Let's go upstairs,' he said.

In a dream she let him lead her back to the lift, his fingers tightly laced in hers. When they reached her room he turned the key and followed her inside.

'Soft lights and sweet music,' he said, 'the infallible recipe. That was my mistake yesterday, trying to rush you. Well, not this time, little one.' He had pulled off his tie and was unbuttoning his shirt. 'This time we both know exactly what we want.'

Natalie stood watching him, a fluttering at the base of her throat as her uncertainties returned. If only he'd say, even untruthfully, that he loved her.

As her immobility reached him he turned sharply and she saw his first doubt. 'What's the matter?' He came slowly towards her, eyes searching her face. 'You're not still pretending, surely? I thought we'd settled that. You're my wife and this is our honeymoon.'

She said with an effort, 'It's not quite as simple as that.'

'I can think of nothing simpler. Believe it or not, this is what we're expected to do!'

'Except that we agreed not to.'

'But it's different now, can't you see that?' A note of impatience, mental as well as physical, crept into his voice. 'Since people know we're married we'll be living under the same roof. You don't imagine we can keep up this genteel celibacy indefinitely?' He looked at her with mounting exasperation. 'Look, I'm not proposing a life-long commitment. It's simply that while we're together, we might as well enjoy ourselves.'

She said very clearly, 'I can't, Roderick. I'm sorry. I thought I could but I can't.'

His eyes narrowed. 'You can, my girl, and you will. I've had enough of this blowing hot and cold.' His hands, no longer gentle, pulled her against him, and with every ounce of willpower she forced herself not to respond. He was holding her so tightly that she couldn't have moved had she wanted to—and she didn't. Abjectly she wanted to stay close to him for ever, which wasn't at all what he had in mind. It was acceptance of this fact that gave her the strength to stand passively while his savage kisses punished her for withstanding him yet again.

At last she felt his arms slacken. He lifted his head and stared down into her face, the breath tearing at his lungs. 'Do you enjoy doing this to me?' he demanded harshly.

She shook her head. 'I'm sorry,' she said again.

'So you should be.' He took a deep breath and his arms fell away from her. 'Suppose I were to insist on my conjugal rights?'

She raised her head. 'Are you going to?'

For a moment he stared at her, at the wide, vulnerable eyes, the trembling mouth bruised from his kisses. 'No,' he said shortly. 'I've never had to force a woman in my life, and I don't intend to start now.'

He retrieved his jacket and tie from the chair where he'd thrown them. 'There can't be many men who return from honeymoon without having slept with their wives.'

'You married the wrong one,' she said aridly.

'So it would seem.' He stopped and looked back at her. 'No, that's not fair. You helped me out on certain conditions, and I've only myself to blame if I now have difficulty keeping them. You shouldn't be so bloody attractive, that's all.'

The door closed behind him and she stood for a long while where he'd left her, waiting for her pulses to stop their clamouring. Then, moving like a sleep-walker, she began to prepare for bed.

CHAPTER SEVEN

Natalie woke to rain drumming on the windows. A thick misty drizzle blotted out the hills and on the terrace below pools of water formed depressingly on the table-tops.

The atmosphere at breakfast was strained. 'What are the arrangements for tomorrow?' she asked, when the lengthening silence became an embarrassment.

'We'll leave after breakfast and be home by

mid-morning. I want a word with the doctor and we'll have an hour or two with Father. Then, after lunch, Drummond can drive us to the airport.' He glanced at her briefly. 'I'm sorry about the penthouse, but there's really no alternative. You'll appreciate it doesn't fit in with my plans, either.'

But he could still go to Isabel's, she reflected, and the thought brought no consolation.

'We can at least be thankful there are two bedrooms,' he added caustically. 'I shouldn't have relished sleeping on the sofa.'

When they came out of the dining-room, groups of guests were standing disconsolately in the hall staring out at the unrelenting weather.

'Natalie!'

She turned, aware of Roderick's annoyance, as Steve came towards them.

'We're fixing a table-tennis tournament for this afternoon. Can we put your name down? And yours too, sir, if you'd like to join in.'

Roderick said heavily, 'I might trip over my stick.'

Steve looked nonplussed and Natalie explained quickly, 'He didn't appreciate the "sir", Steve! As you gathered, this is my husband, Roderick.'

The young man flushed and held out his hand, which Roderick reluctantly took. 'Sorry—I didn't think. Will you join us?'

'Thank you, but no. I've some letters

to write.'

'You'll play, though, won't you, Natalie? Can I have your surname?'

Embarrassed by Roderick's silence, she answered automatically, 'Blair.' She drew in her breath and turned to him quickly but he shook his head. Steve, busily writing on his pad, had noticed nothing.

'Fine. I'll let you know when everything's ready. And if you change your mind, Mr Blair, we can always fit you in.'

'I'm sorry,' Natalie said as he hurried off in search of more recruits.

'Don't be. It's an occupational hazard on honeymoons, and in your case more understandable than most.'

'If you'd rather I didn't play—'

'My dear Natalie, you must do as you like. The most jealous of husbands couldn't object to a tournament on a wet afternoon.'

Nevertheless, when lunch was over he excused himself and went up to his room, ostensibly showing no interest in the proceedings. Pushing him from her mind, Natalie devoted her attention to the game and spent an energetic and enjoyable afternoon. It was almost six when the tournament finished and suddenly it seemed a long time since she'd seen Roderick.

Hoping he hadn't resented her absence, she hurriedly changed for dinner and went to tap on his door. He opened it wearing shorts and a

102

towel slung round his neck.

'Oh, I'm sorry, I—'

'Come in. I'm not wearing any less than I do at the pool.' He tossed the towel through the open bathroom door. 'What can I do for you?'

'I—just wondered how you'd spent the afternoon. It doesn't matter, I'll came back when you're ready.' She turned to the door but his voice halted her.

'Stop behaving like a Victorian governess. I shan't be long.' He took a clean shirt from a drawer and shrugged it on. Trying not to look at him, she inspected the room instead. It was a mirror-image of her own, yet his personal belongings scattered round gave it an entirely different appearance. He was watching her embarrassment with sardonic amusement.

'My afternoon was pleasant, if uneventful, thank you for asking. Did you have a good game?'

'Yes, thank you. It was—great fun.'

'I hope you're still in a competitive mood, because there's a whist drive this evening. I thought we might go along, since it wouldn't be wise to risk the ballroom again.' He was fastening his cuffs, but he shot her a quick look, noting her heightened colour with satisfaction. 'This is, provided you don't regard whist as an old fogey's game?'

'Not at all. I used to play with my parents when I was small.'

'Fine. Well, if you're ready we'll go down for

the last, riotous evening of our honeymoon.'

'Roderick—'

'Joke, my dear. J-O-K-E. All right?'

But Natalie did not enjoy the evening. She found herself continually looking round the room to check where Roderick was. Several times she saw him laughing with his partners, and by the end of the evening he appeared more mellow and relaxed than he'd been since the wedding. This would be the last evening without the threat of Isabel in the background and they hadn't even spent it together. He was still talking to an animated brunette who had been his last partner. Natalie went determinedly across and threaded her arm through his.

'Hello, darling. How did you get on?'

'Quite creditably, I think. At least I didn't disgrace myself. How about you?'

'All right. I haven't added it up.'

He glanced at her card. 'More than all right, by the look of it. That's a sizeable score you have there. You must be in the running for a prize.'

'Really?' Natalie was more interested in the dark girl, who still hovered nearby, but when the highest scores were called out she had indeed won, and to enthusiastic applause went over to Steve to receive a box of chocolates and a kiss on the cheek.

She knew the latter would not please Roderick, but on her return he merely slipped an arm round her shoulder and said casually, 'Congratulations, darling.' The dark girl, accepting defeat at last, moved away and Natalie remained in the circle of Roderick's arm while the second and third prizes were distributed. The evening was over and with it the honeymoon Mrs Downie had insisted on. She could never have imagined the strains and stresses which it had encompassed.

The lift was crowded and it wasn't until Natalie and Roderick emerged on their own floor that he said quietly, 'Now, what was all that about?'

'What do you mean?'

'That little display of wifely jealousy down there.'

She said evenly, 'I was instructed to be loving.'

'You don't usually respond to that instruction.'

'You didn't like Steve kissing me, did you?' she challenged him.

'No.'

The simple confirmation surprised her. 'Why not?'

'Because you're my wife and he's had his eye on you all week.' He smiled slightly. 'So we were both being possessive, which, in the circumstances, is interesting.' They had reached her door and stopped. 'Do I get a good-night kiss?'

With Isabel on hand, it might be the last time

he asked her. 'All right, as long as—'

'—I keep to the rules? Point taken.'

A group of people came round the corner of the corridor. Roderick took the key from her hand, opened the door and they went in. Memories of the previous evening rushed at them from all sides and for a moment they stood in silence looking at each other. Then he put his hands on her shoulders and drew her towards him. His mouth was tender and searching and he was careful not to pull her too close. Her arms had gone instinctively round his neck but after a minute he gently removed them.

'And it is at this point, I think, that I take my leave. Unless,' he added, as she neither moved nor spoke, 'you'd like me to stay?' Wordlessly she shook her head. 'Of course not. Stupid of me. Good night.' And she was alone.

They left the hotel immediately after breakfast. The countryside, newly washed with rain, glowed gold and green under a tremulous sun and clouds were racing across the sky. Within an hour they had reached the outskirts of Edinburgh and soon afterwards were drawing up outside the grey house in Ravelstone Place. Considering she'd spent less than ten days there, it felt surprisingly like home. As Roderick opened the door, Bessie Drummond came hurrying to meet them, her face wreathed in smiles. No bad news, then.

'Welcome back, sir, madam. Would you go

to the library, if you please?'

'The library, Bessie? We were going straight up to Father.'

'The library first, Mr Roddy, if you please.'

With a shrug, Roderick opened the library door. Seated in one of the deep armchairs was Mr McLaren, fully dressed and with a rug across his knees. Roderick stopped in surprise, but Natalie ran past him and dropped to her knees by the old man.

'How lovely to see you downstairs, Father! Are you feeling better?'

He reached for her and pulled her against his bony chest. 'Aye, lassie, right enough, and better still for seeing you. How are you, my boy?' And he reached across her head to take Roderick's hand.

'This is a surprise. How long have you been down?'

'Och well, having proved I was able to get to the wedding, it seemed stupid to spend my days locked away up the stairs. I can rest well enough here and Bessie's been wheeling me like a bairn up and down the pavement in the sunshine. I sent yon other woman packing. Never fear, I'm not going to die yet awhile. I've something to live for now.' And he patted Natalie's shoulder.

Avoiding her husband's eye, she pulled up a chair and they sat down while the old man asked about the hotel. 'By the way,' he told them, 'I've some news for you. You'll not be going to London today.' They stared at him and he added succinctly, 'Strike. Ground staff walked out half an hour ago. It was on the news.'

'How long is it likely to last?'

'Only twenty-four hours, so there's no problem. Bessie's prepared the main bedroom for you.'

Natalie caught and held her breath. Roderick said quickly, 'That's not necessary; there are the rooms we had before.'

'What are you thinking of, boy? A wife of less than a week and you speak of separate rooms?'

Natalie said, 'I didn't sleep well last night. Perhaps it would be better—'

'You'll sleep well enough here. It's a grand bed, that one. Now—' as Roderick started to speak—'I'll hear no more about it. I don't hold with these modern ideas. Sleep together, stay together, I always say. Now, how about a wee drink before dinner? And there's a packet for you on the lobby shelf.'

Roderick went to see to the drinks and returned with the packet, which he tossed on Natalie's lap. 'The photographs, by the look of it.'

She could remember little of her wedding day and it was like looking at a stranger to see the girl in her while dress with Roderick, for the most part unsmiling, by her side.

'By the way, Father,' Roderick was handing

him a glass, 'were you responsible for that write-up in *The Scotsman*?'

'Not at all. They spotted it in the register and phoned for confirmation. Bessie gave them as little as possible but they got on to your London friends, seemingly. Never mind, it might sell you a few more story books!'

After the mid-day meal Mr McLaren settled in his chair for a nap and Roderick and Natalie went to inspect their accommodation. It was a pleasant room with a four-poster in the middle of it. Roderick said, 'Father moved out when my mother died and it's hardly been used since. Don't look so worried, I shan't force my attentions on you. I'll sneak up an easy chair and make use of that.'

'But they'll notice, surely? What will they think?'

'What the hell they like. Unless you'd prefer me to share your bed? I thought not. Bloody ground staff!' he added under his breath.

A quick look in their previous rooms revealed stripped beds and bare mattresses. There was no alternative there.

The doctor called during the afternoon and Sally showed him into the drawing-room, where Roderick and Natalie were relaxing with the papers. 'Well, Mr McLaren, what do you think of your father? Isn't he amazing? I wouldn't have believed it possible, but with proper care there's no reason why he shouldn't last for years. If you'll forgive me saying so, we've your wife to thank.' He smiled kindly at Natalie. 'He thinks the world of her. Now he's all set for—but it's early days yet, and I've no wish to embarrass the young lady!'

Roderick said with an effort, 'Should he be out of his room? I thought stairs were a strain on the heart?'

'They would be, but his man carries him down in the morning and back at night. Mind, the way he's going, he'll soon be racing up and down himself! Now, if you'll excuse me I'll have a word with my patient.'

As the door closed behind him. Natalie said, 'You're in a cleft stick, aren't you? As long as he's alive you're stuck with me.'

'We could try telling the truth, but if the doctor's right and the improvement's largely due to you, your departure may put an end to it.'

'I can't believe I'm that important.'

'You are to him.' He couldn't know how his words hurt her. 'I told you he'd despaired of my marrying. Now,' he added bitterly, 'he's apparently prepared to sit it out waiting for a grandchild, and we know how likely that is. Still, that problem is at least long-term. The immediate worry is that I can't keep you with me indefinitely. You've your own life to lead and can't be expected to sacrifice it for a self-willed old man, however fond you are of him.'

To Natalie's relief, they were interrupted by the arrival of Elizabeth Downie with their wedding present, an old print of Holyrood with Salisbury Crags in the background, and after it had been exclaimed over, and the merits of the hotel recounted, they went through for tea with Mr McLaren.

'Have you asked them about your visit?' the old man enquired of his sister.

'No, Dougal, I really don't think—'

'Nonsense woman, it's the ideal solution.' He turned to Roderick. 'Your aunt's to be in London at the end of the month and she's unwilling to ask you to put her up.'

'But why, Aunt? You always stay with me.'

'It's different now, Roderick. You don't want me butting in so soon, and I can easily—'

'Nonsense.' Roderick stopped suddenly, and Natalie realized he'd remembered the bedroom arrangements.

'Really, I insist. I shan't be far away, and I hope Natalie will come shopping with me and so on, but I do feel that on this occasion I shouldn't intrude further. Please let's leave it at that.'

'Very well,' Roderick said after a pause. 'Let us know the dates when you finalize them and I'll book for a show.'

The fire was lit in the early evening. It was cool in the stone house and the old man felt the chill. When he eventually nodded off to sleep, Roderick rang for Drummond to take him upstairs and soon afterwards Mrs Downie also left.

'You go on up,' Roderick told Natalie. 'I'll bring one of the chairs in a few minutes when I'm not likely to meet anyone on the landing.'

By the time he arrived she was in bed, the linen sheet up to her chin, and she watched him anxiously as he angled the wide-armed chair through the doorway. 'I put a blanket on the stool.'

He glanced at it without comment, searched in his case for the towelling robe, and went with it to the bathroom. The sheets smelled of lavender, and the top one had a wide lace border. Mrs Drummond must have chosen it specially, and her romantic kindness emphasized the gulf which in reality existed between them.

Roderick came back and switched off the light, but moonlight filtered through the thin curtains. Natalie watched as he positioned a pillow and settled himself in the chair, pulling the blanket round him.

'Will you be all right?'

'No doubt I'll survive.'

She lay still, listening to his restless movements as he tried to find a comfortable position. Once she heard the pillow fall to the floor and he swore softly under his breath. It occurred to her that she wasn't going to sleep any better than he did.

Across the silent streets a church clock chimed twelve. Roderick turned again, grabbing for the pillow as it started another

112

descent. 'Shall I try the chair for a while, and let you get some sleep?' Natalie offered.

'I have a better suggestion,' he replied, and she didn't pursue the subject. She fell into an uneasy sleep but, unused to sharing a room, his every movement disturbed her and when she woke to daylight she knew, though it was still early, that she wouldn't sleep again. She lay for what seemed a long time listening to Roderick's deep, even breathing and turning over in her mind the problems that awaited them in London.

At a quarter to eight, aware of noises in the house, she said softly, 'Roderick?'

He opened his eyes at once, grimaced and straightened, rubbing his neck.

'I think tea's on its way.'

He eased himself out of the chair, stretching and yawning.

'How did you sleep?'

'How do you suppose? I'm stiff as hell.' There was a tap on the door and he went to open it, taking the tray from Sally. 'Well,' he commented, setting it down on the table by the bed, 'that's the first time I've shared a room with a woman from a distance of eight feet.'

'At least we spent the night together, which should satisfy your father.' She paused and added, '"Sleep together, stay together".'

'Father has a knack of misquoting when it suits him. The correct phrase is "*Pray* together, stay together", which is equally inapplicable.'

He pulled a pillow into position behind her. 'I'll say this for you, Mrs McLaren, you look as good first thing in the morning as the rest of the time.'

'Thank you,' she said demurely, taking the cup and saucer.

He smiled, stirring his tea. 'I wonder if I'd have co-opted you if you'd been fair, fat and forty? Probably not, since it wouldn't have hoodwinked Father. As it is you have his unqualified approval—and there, as they say, is the rub.'

When Roderick phoned the airport after breakfast he was assured that full services had been resumed. Their honeymoon was officially over. Drummond drove them back along the familiar road to Turnhouse, and Natalie wondered sadly if she'd ever come to Edinburgh again. Though her stay there had been brief, it had included the most momentous days of her life.

CHAPTER EIGHT

Breaking the silence as they drove along the M4, Roderick said: 'I suggest we go straight to Brunswick House, unpack and see if there's anything urgent in the mail. Then I'll take you round to your flat to collect your things.'

'I can't be in and out in five minutes,' Natalie objected. 'I owe them some sort of explanation.'

'Then I'll drop you and pick you up later.'

The penthouse was as luxurious as ever and Natalie realized she must now, at least temporarily, think of it as home. She watched Roderick as he stood flicking through the mail, and her apprehension deepened. In this business setting he had immediately reverted from husband to employer.

'We've certainly created a furore,' he commented. 'The over-riding emotion seems to be one of shock! We'll have to—'

The phone interrupted him. He straightened and turned slightly away from her. 'Hello, Isabel. Yes, five minutes ago. Not today, I'm afraid, there's too much to sort out. I know, but I can't see—Just a minute.' He put his hand over the phone. 'What time do you want to go to the flat?'

'When they get back from work. I'll ring and check it's convenient.'

'Could you eat there, and I'll call back for you later?'

'Of course,' she answered stiffly.

He said into the phone, 'Very well, just after six. We can have dinner.'

During the afternoon Natalie phoned Polly at work. It was a busy office and the conversation, with Roderick witness to one end of it, was fortunately brief.

'Impress on them to be discreet,' he said tersely. 'We don't want the press to get

115

wind of anything.'

'I'm surprised you haven't heard from them.'

'The number's ex-directory. By the way, you're still prepared to work for me, aren't you?'

She looked at him in surprise. 'Was there any doubt? Sarah—'

'I wasn't thinking of "Sarah", but of Aunt Elizabeth, who probably won't approve.'

'But if the flat's cleaned by contract and you eat downstairs, whatever would I do? I'd have to have a job of some kind.'

'My dear girl, I'm not arguing. God knows, we have enough complications without introducing more.'

Natalie was not looking forward to meeting her flatmates. 'I'll be back about nine,' Roderick told her as he drew up outside the familiar house. 'We both need an early night.'

She went up the steps with her head high. He had three hours with Isabel ahead of him, and she preferred not to think how he'd spend them.

Jill opened the door. 'Well, well, if it's not the runaway bride!'

Polly gave her a quick hug. 'You've some explaining to do, my girl! We couldn't believe our ears when we heard it on the news.'

Natalie's eyes widened. 'The wedding was reported on the radio?'

'And T.V. Your husband's quite a celebrity.'

116

Jill bent forward. 'That's some ring you've got there! Let's have a look!'

Natalie held out Margaret McLaren's ruby.

'It's fantastic!' Polly exclaimed. 'You must be over the moon! Come through and tell us all about it.'

'It won't be what you're expecting,' Natalie warned her.

'That explains a lot,' Polly admitted when she came to an end. 'Such as why you didn't mention your engagement when you sent the rent only days before the wedding. It all seemed terribly romantic.'

'Well, it wasn't.'

'And now, since the old boy's pulled through, you're lumbered with each other indefinitely?'

'It looks like it.'

'Mind you,' Polly added consideringly, 'there are worse people to be lumbered with. He's very dishy. I always drool over him when he's on the box.'

Natalie look at her in surprise. 'I've never seen Roderick on television.'

'Must have been when you were out with Clive. And that's another thing. He was on the phone pretty smartly, and of course we couldn't tell him a thing.'

'Yes, he deserves an explanation. But you'll keep it quiet, won't you? We never realized there'd be all this publicity. I'd meant to come back here and just go on working for Roderick as before.'

After supper the three girls packed Natalie's possessions into cases and boxes. 'We'll keep your room for as long as you want it,' Jill assured her. You might be glad of a bolt-hole. And there's no point in lugging your winter things over there, when the old boy could have a heart attack and pop off any time.'

'You'll introduce us to Roderick, won't you?' Polly urged. 'I want to see if he looks as good in real life!'

Since he came to the door she had her wish, and he chatted to both girls for a few minutes before they all loaded the car. Natalie was amused that even Jill fell victim to his charm. But once they were in the car and, she thought sadly, there was no need to exert himself, he fell silent.

'Did you have a pleasant evening?' she asked brightly.

'"Difficult" would be more accurate description.'

'She hasn't forgiven you?'

'I did not,' he said stiffly, 'ask for forgiveness.' He paused, and added, 'It was heavy-going at first, but I think we straightened things out.'

Which was not what she wanted to hear.

As they carried in the boxes of books and records, the guest room rapidly lost its neat anonymity. 'It looks like a transit camp!' Roderick remarked. 'Well, I'll leave you to sort yourself out. Is there anything else you need? There are towels in the second bathroom, so you can take that over.'

'Everything's fine.'

'Then since we slept badly last night, I suggest we call it a day and we can start fresh tomorrow.'

But their work the next morning was soon interrupted. They had only just begun when the intercom sounded and the hall porter announced the arrival of the press. 'Sorry, sir, but they've heard you're back. Could you spare ten minutes for an interview and some photographs?'

'Might as well get it over. All right, Perkins, send them up.' And to Natalie: 'Switch on the radiant bride look, we're going to be on display.'

It was her first experience as an object of publicity, and she did not enjoy it. But she dutifully stood with Roderick by the window, sat with him on the sofa, and smiled every time she was asked. He did most of the talking, for which she was grateful.

'Yes, it was sudden. No, we hadn't known each other long. Yes, my wife is continuing as my secretary for the moment.'

Only when one rash reporter requested that he 'kiss the bride' did a slight edginess show through. 'I think not,' he said smoothly, and offered no explanation. Perhaps, thought Natalie, Isabel wouldn't approve.

She was soon to discover the extent of Isabel's disapproval. Only a short time after the press had gone, they heard a key in the lock and a minute later she appeared at the sitting-room door. Roderick rose warily to his feet but Natalie remained seated. Across the room the two girls exchange a long, cool look. Though her eyes were on Natalie, it was Roderick Isabel addressed.

'All right, sweetheart, I shan't stay. I see you're busy and I mustn't be greedy, after last night. However, you left this behind and I thought you might be needing it.' 'This' was his gold cigarette lighter.

'Thank you.' He walked forward to claim it and her eyes slid past him back to Natalie.

'Congratulations, my dear, on your rapid promotion. A classic case of being in the right place at the right time.'

'Isabel, please. We've been through all this.'

'I know, my love, but you must admit a marriage of convenience can seldom have been more *in*convenient!' She laughed and laid her hand on Roderick's arm. 'Darling, I *am* distracting you, and it's not fair of me. See me to the door, and I'll leave you to your chaste little wife!'

Stiffly Roderick accompanied her out of the room. Natalie's nails were digging into her palms. She knew as well as if she could see them that Isabel was in his arms. After a moment she heard him murmur something and Isabel's low laugh. The front door closed with a little click and Roderick came back into the room. Natalie kept her eyes on her pad.

'I'm sorry about that. Tact has never been Isabel's strong suit.'

Tact, Natalie thought, had nothing to do with it. The purpose of Isabel's visit had been to emphasize the claim she still had on Roderick, and her determination to hold on to it.

She said—and her voice was shaking—'She still has the key to the flat.'

'She's not likely to hand it back.'

Natalie met his eyes. This was the first test and she could not shirk it. 'Then would you please ask for it?' She saw his eyes narrow and went on quickly, 'For better or worse, I'm your wife at the moment, and this is my home. I don't want her here. What you do outside is, of course, your own affair.'

He held her gaze and she saw his surprise and a grudging respect. 'Very well,' he said quietly. 'For as long as we're married, she won't come here again. I give you my word.'

'Thank you.'

'I know she hurt you,' he went on, 'and I'm sorry, but try to see her viewpoint. After going round together for some time, I suddenly go off and marry someone else. She can't even tell people it's not what it seems.' He paused. 'And presumably friend Clive feels the same. How will he react to our photographs in the paper?'

121

'I've been putting it off,' Natalie said, 'but I'll have to go and see him. And Sarah, too.'

'Then I suggest you go to the office and make your phone calls while I look through the draft for the next chapter.'

The call to Clive took all her courage. Since the direct approach seemed best, she simply said, 'It's Natalie, Clive. Could I possibly see you?'

There was a long silence, then he said baldly, 'Why?'

'There are things to explain, and—'

'You're damn right there are, but it's a bit late for explanations.'

Her hand tightened on the receiver. 'Could we meet for a drink this evening?'

'You're in a hurry, after all this time.'

'Please, Clive.'

He said grudgingly, 'I'm playing squash at six, but I suppose I could meet you later, if it's so all-fired important. Eight-thirty at Domino's?'

'That'll be fine.'

Trying not to think of the impending meeting, she dialled Sarah's number.

'Well, Mrs McLaren!' came the mocking tones. 'Do you want to re-engage me as your husband's secretary?'

'Sarah—don't!' Natalie closed her eyes on sudden tears and her cousin's voice changed.

'He, ove, that was a joke! A bit heavy-hand. d perhaps, but you took me by surprise.

And not for the first time, I might add! I was completely shattered when I heard of the wedding. You might have told me, specially since I played Cupid and brought you together.'

'Will you just be quiet a minute and listen?' Wearily she repeated the story she'd told Jill and Polly. 'But no one must find out,' she finished, 'or it'll all have been a waste of time. I want to see you, but at the moment things are pretty hectic. How's your arm?'

'Improving, thanks. The splint came off a couple of days ago and I'm having physiotherapy.' She paused. 'I'm still trying to take in what you told me. It sounds very high-handed, but typical, of course, when we know how he regards women. Stand-in secretary, why not stand-in wife?'

'Yes,' said Natalie bleakly. 'Look, Sarah, I have to go. I'll be in touch.' She put the phone down and sat with bent head. She'd forgotten how well Sarah knew Roderick, but her assessment of the situation was depressingly accurate.

'You've fixed it?' he asked from the doorway.

She looked up, brushing a hand across her eyes, and his brows drew together. 'Won't he see you?'

'Yes, we're meeting for a drink this evening.' So you're free to go back to Isabel. She caught her lip between her teeth.

123

Roderick said gently, 'It's important to you, isn't it? Would you like me to see him first, and explain?'

She shook her head. 'No, I can manage,' she said.

But when, a few hours later, she saw Clive waiting for her at their favourite wine bar, Natalie's nerve almost failed her. He stood watching her approach and his eyes were hard. She saw them flicker to her left hand.

'Shall we sit down?' She moved to a table with no one else nearby and he followed with some wine and glasses.

'You're certainly a fast worker when it suits you,' he said. 'Stupid of me not to have twigged it was money that turned you on. I hope he's got enough to make him worth sleeping with.'

Her face flamed. 'That's what I want to explain. I haven't slept with him, Clive.'

He stared at her, his face stiff with disbelief. 'You're trying to tell me you haven't been to bed with your husband?'

'That's exactly what I'm telling you.'

'You mean the poor devil's got no further than I did? My God, Natalie—'

'You were right on one point,' she interrupted. 'Money came into it, but not in the way you think. It's—simply a business arrangement, and in due course there'll be a settlement.' She could see on his face a mirror of her own distaste. 'But that wasn't why I agreed to it,' she went on in a low voice. 'It was

124

because his father's dying and had set his heart on being at his son's wedding. There's more to it, but that's the gist of it.' Her hands were clenched on the table. 'Please, Clive—it's important that you believe me.'

There was a long silence while he digested what she had told him.

'There'll be pictures in the paper tomorrow. That's why I had to see you now.'

He let out his breath on a long sigh. 'I shouldn't have said what I did. I was trying to hurt you.'

'I understand.'

'It was like a slap in the face, hearing you were married. God, I'd only just got your note from Scotland, and there was no hint in that. You can't wonder I was bitter. And hurt. I wish I'd known the truth, though.' He gave a twisted smile. 'You know what they say about the rebound.'

'You've found someone else?' Natalie tried to keep the hope out of her voice.

'In a manner of speaking. But—'

She reached forward and took his hand. 'Clive, I didn't ask you to meet me so we could start up again. We couldn't, anyway, for some time yet, and it's not fair to expect you to wait.'

The long-lashed eyes were on her face. 'If I thought I'd a chance in hell with you, I'd drop her. But I haven't, have I, Natalie?'

'No,' she said softly. 'Not in the way you want.'

125

With the air cleared between them, they had little else to say to each other and after a few minutes finished their drinks and separated. It had been a traumatic day and Natalie was glad it was over. But it wasn't—quite.

Roderick came into the hall as she entered the flat. Having assumed he'd be out, she was surprised to see him and felt her control slipping. 'Good night,' she said hurriedly, and tried to pass him, but he caught hold of her.

'What happened? Didn't he believe you? You should have let me—' His voice sharpened. 'You're not crying?'

'I don't think so!' She gave a tremulous little laugh.

'Oh God, Natalie, I'm sorry. Let me get you a drink.'

'No, really, I'd rather—' But he was leading her through to the sitting-room. It was in darkness except for a pool of light from the lamp at one end of the sofa.

'It's been one hell of a day for you. Just relax for a few minutes.'

He went to the drinks cabinet and she sat down and closed her eyes. 'Aunt Elizabeth phoned. She's booked in at the Capital for a week from the twenty-fifth—that's a fortnight tomorrow. She wanted to speak to you, of course.'

'What did you say?'

'That you were visiting friends. It seemed better to opt for the plural.' He handed her a glass and she took a quick gulp and choked, looking up accusingly.

'This isn't sherry!'

'I felt you were in need of something stronger.' He sat beside her and almost absent-mindedly took her hand. 'I gather Clive didn't give you an easy time?'

She remembered his own words concerning Isabel. 'We straightened it out in the end.' It wasn't safe to sit in the dimness holding his hand. In her weakened state she was capable of burying her face in his chest, and as he'd said earlier, they had enough complications. She finished her drink quickly and rose to her feet.

'Thanks—that should make me sleep!' she said, and if the smile she gave him was shaky, at least it was a smile. Avoiding his keen eyes, she turned and went out of the room.

CHAPTER NINE

The newspaper photographs alerted Roderick's friends to his return to London and a succession of invitations followed—to supper parties, drinks, the theatre. 'Everyone's anxious to meet you,' he told Natalie, 'so we'll have to put a brave face on it. You'd better go along to Harrod's and replenish your wardrobe. If we're required to socialize you can't keep wearing the same dress. Don't worry about the cost; consider it part of the deal if it makes you feel better.'

It was on one of these occasions that she met Roderick's agent, Jonathan Bryce. The tall, bespectacled man smiled down at her. 'I'm delighted to meet you, Mrs McLaren. I've been parading beautiful women in front of Roderick for as long as I can remember to no avail, but I must admit he's come up trumps! I believe you were his secretary?'

'I still am, as a matter of fact.'

'Then if you'll forgive "shop" for a moment, how's the new book coming along?'

'Quite well, I think, but there have been one or two—interruptions.'

He gave a shout of laughter. 'That has to be the understatement of the year! Is it a follow-up to *"Eye of the Storm"*?'

'I'm not sure,' she hedged.

'Well, with that one in line for the Radbrook Award, it would be a good move if it were.'

'Roderick's book's entered for an award?'

He looked surprised. 'You didn't know? Yes, it's well in the running as far as we can tell. I hope it comes off, he deserves it.'

'When will you hear?'

'Middle of next month, with luck. That's why I'd like the new one in my hands by then, though I can't blame him for not keeping his mind on work at the moment!'

'Mr Bryce was telling me about your book being nominated,' Natalie said later that evening when, back at the flat, she was making

128

some coffee before bed. 'He seems to think it stands a good chance.'

'I hope he's right. It's silly, really, but I've set my heart on winning it.'

Natalie watched the coffee drip through the filter. 'Aren't films and T.V. serials enough?'

'Not,' he said surprisingly, 'to satisfy Father. He pretends to believe they're adapted from badly-written pot-boilers and refuses to be impressed, but even he would admit the prestige of an award. Specially the Radbrook.' He pulled out a chair and sat down. 'It's childish, but I told you I have this compulsion to prove myself to him, and there may not be much more time.'

'Is the new book a sequel?'

He gave a short laugh. 'You don't know much about my work, do you? It is, as it happens.' He looked up at her consideringly. 'Come to think of it, you probably agree with Father. You weren't over-keen on my books yourself.'

She flushed. 'I didn't say that.'

'But you had reservations. What were they?'

'Oh, nothing, really.'

'But I'd like to know.'

She shook her head. 'It's not important.' Without looking at him, she set mugs on the table and poured the steaming black liquid into them. He waited till she'd finished. 'Now,' he said, 'sit down and give me a detailed criticism. It should be most instructive.'

'For goodness' sake, Roderick, can't we drop it? What does it matter what I think, when—'

He reached out, his fingers closing on her wrist. 'Natalie, I'm beginning to lose patience. Will you tell me, or do I have to shake it out of you?'

Her anger rose to meet his. 'All right, since you're so determined to know, I'll tell you. What spoils your books is that the women in them are cardboard dummies! All right, so the plots are exciting, but the characters need to be convincing, too, and the heroines are as interchangeable as a set of robots!'

She broke off, seeing his mouth tighten. The only sound in the room was her rapid breathing.

'Please go on.'

Rashly, she obeyed him. 'You don't seem to realize they have minds as well as bodies. All they think about is the quickest way to get to bed!'

'Which I find true of most women.' His voice was silken. 'You, my dear, are the exception which proves the rule.'

'If you believe that, you don't know much about women.'

'I think,' he said curtly, 'that I can claim some experience. And you can take off that Sunday School expression. Despite what you may think, I'm not a complete egoist. When I make love, I try to give as much pleasure

130

as I receive.'

'But "making love" isn't the right phrase, is it? Love never enters into it.'

'What's the difference? As the song has it, "the fundamental things apply".' His eyes went over her flushed face. 'Have you ever been in love?'

The challenge took her by surprise, but she answered honestly. 'Yes.'

'Then you can instruct me on the finer points. In the interest of art, naturally.' He rose to his feet and pulled her to hers. 'How, for instance, does a loving kiss differ from the merely self-gratifying? Would you care to demonstrate?'

'No, thank you.'

'But presumably when I kissed you, you detected the difference?'

'Oh, yes!' she said ringingly.

His fingers tightened on her arm. 'Very well, then. Lesson 1. I'd like you to use all your acting ability and kiss me as if you loved me.'

She looked up at him, the breath clogging in her throat. 'Roderick, this has gone far enough. I knew you wouldn't accept criticism, that was why—'

'My dear, I not only accept it, I'm trying to profit from it. A life-like heroine in one of my books—just imagine! You owe it to posterity!'

Natalie hadn't realized quite how angry he was. 'I'm sorry,' she said numbly. 'You made me tell you, I didn't want to.' She tried to free herself from his hold.

'Please let me go.'

'You're going to kiss me, Natalie, whether you like it or not. If you go to your room I shall simply follow you. There are no locks on the doors.'

Her voice shook. 'Then Lesson 1 is that you can't force someone to kiss you "as if she loved you".'

'Point taken, but please try. The sooner you start, the sooner it will be over.' He was standing motionless, his face a mask. Since she'd no choice she slipped her arms round his neck and kissed him. A tremor went through him but he didn't move, and suddenly all the love she'd been suppressing came rushing to the surface. Her arms tightened and she pressed herself closer, parting his lips with her own. He was still angry with her, unwilling to respond, but gradually his arms closed round her and as he took over the initiative the tenor of the kiss altered, becoming potentially dangerous. Natalie turned her head and his lips moved over her jawline.

'I can think of a more suitable place for this demonstration,' he murmured in her ear.

She pulled herself free. 'Sorry, that's well beyond the scope of Lesson 1!' She tried to laugh, but there was a hard knot in her chest and she couldn't breathe.

He said urgently, 'Natalie, you know how much I want you.'

132

'Yes,' she answered unevenly. 'But if this was for real, you'd say you loved me.' For a moment longer their eyes held. Then she said, 'Good night, Roderick,' and walked blindly from the room.

*   *   *

When she went for her bath the next morning, Natalie could hear his voice in the sitting-room and realized he was dictating into the machine. It was barely eight o'clock.

'Breakfast?' she enquired from the doorway half an hour later.

He didn't look up. 'Just coffee, please. I've been here since six. There's a cassette on your desk.'

The mugs of cold black coffee were still on the kitchen table. Natalie poured them away and made fresh. She took a cup into Roderick and carried her own through to the office, no more anxious for his company than he seemed to be for hers.

But she had only been typing a short time before a sense of familiarity intruded. She sat back, letting the cassette run on for several minutes while he dictated, flatly and unemotionally, a scene almost identical to the one that had taken place in the hotel bedroom.

Trembling with a sense of betrayal, she stormed back to the sitting-room. 'I can see why you didn't dictate that personally!' she

133

began without preamble.

He turned from a contemplation of the view. 'Does it come across all right?'

She stared at him accusingly. 'How could you do it? Haven't you any sense of decency?'

'There's no pleasing you, is there? You complain my heroines are lifeless, but when I take something from life, you object to that, too.'

'So it was revenge for last night! I didn't know you could be so vindictive!'

He said tightly, 'I'm a writer, my dear, and we're known for a certain ruthlessness. It's all grist to the mill. Now will you please return to your typing and let me get on!'

'I'm not going to do it!'

His eyes glinted. 'I think you are.' He saw her lip tremble and added more gently, 'Look, we know it actually happened, but no one else will. What harm can it do?'

'It's—degrading.'

'If anyone was degraded,' he said curtly, 'it certainly wasn't you. Now please go. You're interrupting my train of thought.'

She stayed in the office all morning, typing with a speed and accuracy born of anger. At half-past twelve Roderick came to the door. 'Ready for lunch?'

'No.'

'Stop sulking, there's a good girl. You'd no breakfast and you need something to eat.'

Mutinously she pushed the machine aside

and went to join him. He put an arm round her, pulling her briefly to his side. 'And for the record, I didn't mean to hurt your feelings. It just seemed to fit, and I could vouch for its authenticity.'

They went down in the lift in silence but as they came out of the building Roderick said, 'I've a T.V. recording this afternoon. Would you like to come?'

'No, thank you.'

'For God's sake, Natalie!'

'I met enough people last night. I couldn't face any more at the moment.'

'Very well, suit yourself. I was trying to spare you a solitary afternoon.'

'It needn't be solitary. I'll take the opportunity to go and see Sarah.'

It was a relief to part from him when lunch was over. Natalie caught a bus and sat staring out of the window at the moving throngs. The day was warm and overcast and looked like rain. It hadn't occurred to her to bring an umbrella. As she swung off the bus, she thought suddenly: Suppose Sarah's not at home? Mentally crossing her fingers, she rang the doorbell.

It was answered almost at once. 'Thank goodness you're in!' Natalie said. And burst into tears.

Five minutes later they were sitting in the pocket handkerchief that Sarah called her garden. The surroundings were not inspired, being composed of fire-escapes and the backs of buildings, but at least it was private.

'I'm sorry,' Natalie said, drying her eyes. 'I was in need of that and there's no privacy at home.'

Sarah's round face was full of concern. 'What's the matter, love? Is he being more difficult than usual?'

Natalie managed a weak smile. 'I told him last night what I thought of his heroines.'

Sarah gave an exaggerated gasp. 'And you're alive to tell the tale?'

'Only just.'

'What did he say?'

'That he'd had more women than I'd had hot dinners and knew what he was talking about.'

'He might have a point there.'

'Indeed.'

Sarah looked at her keenly for a moment and then said flatly, 'So help *me*, you're in love with him!'

'So help *me*!' Natalie tried to laugh but it was more like a sob. 'I'm an idiot, aren't I?'

'When did this happen?'

'I only realized on our honeymoon.'

'He hasn't—?'

'No, but not for want of trying.'

'Why don't you let him, if you love him?'

'Because he doesn't love me. Yes, I know it's a stupid reason, but it's the best I can come up with.'

'How's his father?'

136

'Flourishing, from all accounts.'

'So this could go on indefinitely?'

'Unless Roderick decides his father's strong enough to take it.'

Sarah said worriedly, 'I feel so responsible. I got you into this, but heaven knows how I can get you out.'

'The trouble is, I don't want to get out.' A large drop of rain fell like a sympathetic tear.

'Uh—uh! We'd better get inside before the heavens open. You didn't bring a coat, did you?'

They stood together at the window of Sarah's flat while the rain sluiced down, deluging the area where they'd been sitting, streaming down the iron stairs, cascading into the drainpipes. A brilliant flash lit up their faces, followed almost at once by a peal of thunder.

'Did you say when you'd be back?'

'No, we weren't communicating too well. Roderick's doing a T.V. recording this afternoon.'

'He could be some time, then. Why not stay for a meal? My flat-mate won't be back till late and you certainly can't go home till the rain eases. Any coat of mine would swamp you.'

They shared a T.V. dinner out of Sarah's minute freezer. It reminded Natalie of similar occasions at Tavistock Mews. For the last week she and Roderick had been dining in the Brunswick restaurant and it was pleasant to relax in front of the television with trays on their knees. The storm had passed, and at eight o'clock Natalie set off for home.

But the rain started again as she waited for a bus, and by the time she reached the penthouse she was wet and shivering. As her key made contact with the lock, the door swung open and Roderick stood there.

'Where the hell have you been?'

'Sarah's. I told you.'

He frowned, looking her over. 'How did you get so wet?'

'I had to wait some time for a bus.'

'A *bus*? Good God, why didn't you take a taxi? I don't expect my wife to wait at bus-stops!'

'Your wife,' she said clearly, 'is going for a hot bath, if you'll excuse me.'

He was waiting for her when she emerged from the bathroom. 'I've made a hot toddy. You'd better drink it.'

She followed him to the sitting-room. He'd switched on an electric fire and drawn a chair up to it, and she was touched by his concern.

'Have you eaten?' he asked, handing her the drink.

'Yes, at Sarah's. Have you?'

'No, I was waiting for you.'

'Oh Roderick, I'm sorry, but it was raining so hard and Sarah said you'd be some time at the Centre. Why don't you go down now?'

'I'm not hungry. I'll open a tin of soup later.'

'If we'd anything in the fridge I could make you something. I haven't cooked for weeks, I quite miss it.'

'We can eat here any time you like.' He was still watching her warily.

She cupped her hands round the hot mug. 'How did the show go?'

'All right.'

'I've never seen the programme. When will it be on?'

'Next week sometime. Tuesday, I think. They were disappointed you didn't come along.'

She closed her eyes, letting the warmth seep into her. 'Another time, perhaps.'

He said abruptly, 'I'll alter that chapter, if you like.'

'It's done now. Perhaps I was being over-sensitive.'

A truce seemed to have been reached. If it made for a less emotional existence, Natalie was ready to abide by it.

The days passed slowly. She watched the television programme while Roderick, showing no interest, did some writing at the other end of the room. The questions directed at him were for the most part literary and Natalie was surprised by the breadth of his knowledge. It gave her a glow of pride to listen to his deep voice with its faint Scottish accent giving carefully considered replies. She said suddenly, 'Is it because you live in London that your accent isn't as strong as your father's?'

'Oh, Father's not as broad as he makes out. He puts on his Harry Lauder act for English visitors.'

'Which includes me?'

'It won't when he knows you better.' He paused. 'If he gets the chance.'

Prudently, Natalie returned her attention to the set.

She had decided to cook dinner at home the evening before Mrs Downie's arrival. Roderick had an appointment with his publishers that afternoon, which gave her time for her preparations. There was no dining-room in the penthouse and she did not want to serve the meal in the kitchen, so she carried the hall table through to the sitting-room. But when she came to lay it, it was clear Roderick never ate at home. The only plates were the heavy ironware ones in the kitchen, and its table drawer the sole supply of cutlery.

When Roderick returned, he stopped in surprise in the sitting-room doorway, taking in the table with its wine glasses and the vase of roses in the centre.

'This does look pleasant—almost makes me feel married! Isn't this where you ask if I'd a good day at the office?'

'Did you? At the publishers'?'

'So–so. The Americans are dragging their feet on the paperback deal, which is annoying, but I think they'll come through.'

The meal was a great success and Natalie was amused by Roderick's evident surprise at her skills. 'You might regret this,' he teased her. 'Suppose I decide to eat at home every evening?'

'I'd enjoy it, provided you invested in a table and some decent china.'

'You would? That'd be no problem.'

'Except,' she said, dropping her eyes, 'that it would hardly be worth while.'

'No,' he agreed after a moment. 'I was forgetting.'

'Since we're playing house this evening,' he remarked over coffee, 'I presume I'm expected to help with the dishes?'

'That's not necessary. They won't take long.'

'It would be a novelty—I'd enjoy it.'

Since he insisted she didn't argue, but whether he regarded it as 'playing house' or not, the sharing of so humdrum a task was disturbing. As she was rinsing round the sink, he pushed her hair to one side and kissed the back of her neck.

'Thank you for a lovely evening,' he said, and she was thankful he couldn't see the pain in her eyes.

CHAPTER TEN

It was pleasant to see Elizabeth Downie again. Roderick had booked seats at the theatre for the Tuesday, a new musical comedy, and Natalie remembered Clive having suggested, the last evening they were together, that they might go to see it. In view of which, it should not have been as much of a shock as it was to see him there.

They had gone to the bar in the interval, and while Elizabeth settled herself at a table, Natalie followed Roderick to help him carry back the glasses. He had shouldered his way through the crowd at the bar and she was waiting on the fringe of it when Clive, two glasses and a bottle of tonic in his hands, turned to come away. They saw each other in the same moment and both stopped, jolted on all sides by the people round them.

He said jerkily, 'Natalie! You—look great.'

She forced a smile, trying to ease the sudden tension. 'So do you!' It was true, too. His broad shoulders and tanned, handsome face were causing several turned heads from the girls round about. And since he held two glasses one of them must be with him.

He said, 'We intended coming to this show, remember?'

'Yes, I was just thinking of that.'

'Are you all right?' he asked abruptly. 'I mean, is it working out?'

Behind her, Roderick's voice said sharply, 'Natalie!'

Since there was no help for it, she introduced them while the two men eyed each other with

142

undisguised dislike. Then she took the glass Roderick was handing her and, with a murmured farewell, they moved away.

'So that's the famous Clive!' he said tightly. 'You didn't tell me he was so pretty!'

They had reached the table, so no reply was possible. Elizabeth glanced from Natalie's blushes to her nephew's compressed lips. 'Have you the programme with you, Natalie?' she asked lightly. 'I want to check who's playing the mother.'

Natalie's hands were shaking as she handed over the programme. She'd done nothing wrong, she thought resentfully, and Roderick's reaction was wholly unreasonable. Then, aware of the older woman's calm appraisal, she pushed the incident from her mind and made some comment on the play.

But if she hoped to have diverted Mrs Downie's interest, she had not succeeded. It had been arranged that Natalie should spend the following day shopping with Elizabeth, and it was over lunch that the subject was raised.

'Who was that young man at the theatre?' Elizabeth asked with apparent casualness.

'Someone I used to know.'

'And Roderick was jealous?'

'Not exactly.'

'My dear, I'm a nosy old busybody, but you haven't a mother and I'm fond of you. You don't seem as happy as I'd expected. Is anything wrong?' Natalie didn't answer, and she went on: 'There's something between you and Roderick which I can't define, and it's been worrying me. If it's anything I can help with, I'd like to feel you can confide in me.'

Around them the clatter of plates and the light chatter of the shoppers seemed another world. Elizabeth waited patiently while Natalie crumbled the roll on her plate. Then, coming to a decision, the girl looked up.

'Can you keep a secret?'

'Of course.'

'Two secrets, actually. Roderick might not like me telling you this, but I think I have to. The truth is that when I went up to Scotland, it was quite simply as his secretary. What's more, I'd been working for him less than a week.'

'But—'

'Mr McLaren jumped to the wrong conclusion, that's all. He was so thrilled and delighted and—we thought he was dying.'

'I can't be hearing this,' Elizabeth said slowly.

'It was only supposed to be a white lie, to comfort him. But everything just—took off.'

'You're really telling me—? But this is terrible! I can hardly believe it.' Helplessly Natalie watched her dawning anger. 'And Roderick allowed it to go on—forced you to carry the thing through? It's preposterous! He's always been high-handed, but this!'

'I agreed,' Natalie defended him. 'We

144

didn't realize—'

'I can see—just—that in the first flurry of misunderstanding you kept back the truth. But later, when, God help me, I joined in pressing you to go ahead with the wedding—surely you could have told me then?'

'I think Roderick meant to originally, but you arrived while he was asleep and by the time he came in, you'd met me and heard the news and everything.'

'But this—pandering to Dougal was quite unnecessary. He might be a wilful old man, but he's not a child. Of *course* he'd set his heart on Roderick marrying, and of course he fell for you. He'd have been bitterly disappointed to learn the truth, but it wouldn't have killed him.'

'I realized that later, but by then it was too late.'

'And how long does Roderick propose to keep up this charade? As long as it suits him, I suppose. He's managed to secure a pretty young girl to—' She broke off and Natalie's face flamed.

'I should have made it clear it's in name only.'

'I'm glad of that, at least. Just as well I decided not to stay with you, wasn't it?' Her eyes went over the girl's unhappy face. 'You said there were two secrets?'

'You can probably guess the other.'

'You've fallen for him?' She put her hand

over Natalie's. 'Poor wee thing. I suppose it was inevitable. He's arrogant and dictatorial like his father, but he's a very attractive man. He doesn't know how you feel?'

'No, and he mustn't. It's complicated enough. You're only the second person I've told.'

'You don't think he might be falling for you, too?'

Natalie shook her head decidedly. 'I'm not the type that appeals to him.'

'I shouldn't be too sure.' Elizabeth said reflectively. 'Still, you know best. So that remains a secret between us but you can tell him I know the rest.'

Natalie did so that evening, and as she'd anticipated he was not pleased. 'A bit unnecessary, wasn't it, at this stage?'

'It wasn't my idea, Roderick. She brought up the subject.'

He frowned. 'How could she have done?'

'She noticed the—friction between us last night. But you'd been thinking of telling her, hadn't you?'

'Only at the beginning. She'd never have sanctioned our going ahead with the wedding. Well, it's done now. No doubt I'll get the rough edge of her tongue. She'll see you as a wronged child-bride—which, of course, you are.'

Certainly there was a coolness the next time they met, but Roderick impatiently brushed aside his aunt's strictures. 'There's nothing you can call me that I haven't called myself. Of course I was a fool, and believe me I regret it, but for the moment our hands are tied.'

Natalie turned away and Elizabeth's eyes followed her with sympathy. But all she said was, 'Very well, we'll say no more about it, provided you don't try to force Natalie to stay with you any longer than she wants to. But what about Eagle's Crag? Will you go up there?'

'It'd be difficult to avoid. Father seems set on it.'

Elizabeth turned to Natalie. 'We usually spend some weeks up there at the end of the summer. Dougal and I were brought up on the estate and Roderick grew up there, too, till he went to boarding school. Dougal always hoped he'd take over one day.'

'Instead of writing fairy-stories in London.'

'Well, each to his taste. Fortunately we've a very able factor to look after it in the meantime.'

No more was said about their marriage, but Elizabeth's displeasure lay just below the surface, marring the remainder of her visit. Sadly, it was a relief when she returned home, and their life reverted to what seemed to be its normal pattern. During the day, Roderick and Natalie were constantly together, and though most of the time he treated her quite simply as his secretary, she was finding it increasingly hard to conceal her own feelings. Occasionally in the evening he went out alone, and though he vaguely spoke of 'meetings', Natalie was convinced that he spent those times with Isabel.

She was therefore delighted when Polly phoned, inviting her to join herself and Jill at the cinema the following week. It would be good to relax with her friends without having to watch every word and expression. But before the evening at the cinema an important development took place.

Natalie had decided to cook another meal and during the afternoon slipped out to buy the last few ingredients. When she returned, Roderick was staring out of the sitting-room window, and something in his stance alarmed her. His father—?

She said sharply, 'What's happened?'

He didn't turn. 'Jonathan phoned. Steve Delaney's been awarded the Radbrook Prize.'

She stood motionless, still clutching the carrier-bag. 'Oh, Roderick,' she said softly, 'I'm so sorry.'

'Well, it was always on the cards. I was a fool to pin my hopes on it.'

'But they thought your—'

'Quite, but you never know till the last minute which one will come through.'

'Can I get you anything?'

'No, thanks.' He gave a harsh laugh. 'Don't worry, I shan't jump out of the window!'

The meal was a silent affair. To mask the

lack of conversation, Natalie put on some records. At one point Roderick said, 'I'm afraid I'm not very good company.' Nor, this time, did he help with the dishes, though it wasn't a deliberate omission. He simply didn't think of it.

When she came back from the kitchen he had switched on the television. It was a comedy programme and he seemed to relax and even laughed a couple of times. When it was over, Natalie went to bed and some time later heard Roderick go to his room. But she couldn't sleep. She knew how disappointed he was, and ached to comfort him.

It was a long time later that she heard his door softly open again. She tensed and sat up, listening. A thin line of light showed under the door. She slipped out of bed and quietly turned her own door-knob. The light was coming from the sitting-room, at a guess, the lamp on the drinks cabinet. Bare-footed, she padded across the hall. Roderick was indeed at the cabinet, dropping an ice cube into the glass he held. Though she made no sound, he turned swiftly.

'Are you all right?' she faltered.

'Fantastic.'

She said gently, 'There'll be other prizes.'

'Not in Father's lifetime. If I could just have handed it to him, said, "Surely you can be proud of this?"' He put the glass down abruptly and turned away, staring out into the

149

night-time darkness.

Natalie walked across the room, put her arms round him and laid her face against his back. He jerked as though she'd touched a nerve. The blue robe, familiar as an old friend, was rough under her cheek. 'It's not the end of the world,' she murmured.

Slowly he turned, still in the circle of her arms. He said unevenly, 'I've told you before about following men in your nightdress.'

'Yes,' she answered, 'I know.' Somehow it didn't seem to matter at all. She lifted her face, glorying in the desperation of his kisses, and she knew that this time, though still no word of love had passed between them, she would not draw back. Until now she had been able, with difficultly, to withstand his passion and her own longing, but tonight there was the addition of tenderness, and against that she had no defence.

Nor, when it was over, had she the slightest tremor of regret. She felt cherished, fulfilled, and boundlessly happy. But the emotion that overrode all others was the force of her love—doubled, trebled by the experience they had shared.

She woke slowly to a room full of sunshine, but the other side of the bed was empty and the sheet felt cold to her hand. He must have left as soon as she fell asleep. Why? She sat up, glancing for instinctive reassurance at her wedding-ring. It was all right, she told herself.

Everything was all right. But the cold sheet had brought the first thread of unease. She slipped on her dressing-gown and opened the door, listening. There was no sound and the sitting-room door was shut. She had her bath, dressed, tidied the room. Still no sound, and by now shyness had closed over her. dampening her palms and drying her mouth. What should she say to him?

She went to the kitchen to put on some coffee, and across the hall the sitting-room door opened at last. Her body jerked but she held herself still. 'Hello,' she said softly.

'Natalie.' He spoke her name as though he'd never said it before, was pausing to consider the sound of it. But he did not, as she'd expected, come and take her in his arms. Hardly breathing, she waited, and Roderick said violently, 'What can I say? Damn it, words are my business, but—' He ran a hand through his hair. 'Look, I'm sorry. I lost control. I'd give anything for it not to have happened.'

She was staring at him with an intensity which blurred his features and made her eyeballs ache. Instinctively she held out a hand, but he didn't see it.

'I took advantage of your pity,' he said.

'But it was what you wanted! Look how many times—'

'But not like that. Not because you were sorry for me.'

'That wasn't the reason! I wanted it, too, you

know I did!'

'You'd no trouble resisting me before. Let's not pretend, Natalie. You were sweet and generous and I took advantage of you. And I'm bitterly sorry.'

Behind her, the coffee began to bubble gently and she automatically moved it off the flame. 'Very well,' she said in a hard little voice, 'If that's what you want, I'll try to pretend it never happened.'

'Don't think I'm not grateful. It was—'

'Roderick!' She put both hands to her head. 'No more, please!'

He turned and went back to the sitting-room. She stood rock-still, drawing deep breaths, counting them, forcing herself to think of nothing but the next number.

When she reached twenty, she poured herself a cup of scalding coffee and drank it, still standing where he'd left her. If he wanted a cup, he could come and get it himself.

Face it, she told herself. Face it, then try to forget it. He'd slept with her, yes, but he hadn't been 'making love' as she had. It shouldn't have surprised her; he'd been completely honest about his views. What had he said, that first night in Edinburgh? '. . . if you go running after men in your nightgown, that kind of thing is liable to happen.' Well, as he'd remarked, she had done it again and the inevitable occurred. And the ludicrous part was that it was he who was sorry.

She went into the office and began to type. After a while, Roderick buzzed for her and she went through with her pad. Not looking at him, she sat down, waiting with pencil poised. But he said gently, 'Natalie love, I didn't mean to fling it back in your face.'

'I thought we weren't going to talk about it.' Her voice shook only a little.

'But I can't let you think I blame you. The responsibility was all mine. I knew you'd really no intention of going to bed with me, and I should have respected that, even when your sympathy got the better of you.'

It was pointless to keep repeating that she'd wanted to make love to him. He might realize the truth. So she gave him a tight, blind little smile, and after a moment he said flatly, 'The next chapter, then, if you're ready.'

But his manner towards her had changed. He was at the same time more formal and more considerate, careful not to come closer than necessary in their daily contacts, but seeking to please her in little ways. He couldn't know that this new concern, far from soothing her, made matters worse, emphasizing as it did his persistent sense of guilt. If he'd snapped at her, as he had more than once in the past, it would have been easier to bear than this distanced, impersonal tenderness.

CHAPTER ELEVEN

'I'm going to the cinema with the girls this evening,' Natalie said on the Thursday morning.

'Fine. I'll run you there.'

'Don't bother, I'll get a bus.'

'It's no trouble, and you'll be sure of being on time. Shall I pick you up afterwards?'

'Whatever for?' Aware of sounding ungracious, she added: 'We'll probably go somewhere for a pizza. There won't be time for them to eat beforehand.'

Polly and Jill were outside the cinema when Roderick dropped her. 'Chauffeur service, no less!' Jill teased.

'I'm not sure I don't prefer your Roderick to Jeremy Irons!' Polly said, gazing after the disappearing car. 'I'm beginning to think, Natalie, that we're wasting our sympathy on you!'

It was hot in the cinema and Natalie developed a headache, but the film was enjoyable and afterwards they made their way to a pizzeria. Over the meal she dutifully reeled off the names of the celebrities she'd met at the various parties, and aroused their envy with details of the new wardrobe Roderick had insisted on.

'It'll be rather a come-down, when you're

back with us,' Jill said with her mouth full. 'Any idea yet when it may be?'

'None. We're probably going to Scotland soon. They have an estate in the Highlands.'

'They haven't a spare villa in the south of France, by any chance? We'd be willing to work our passage!'

It was nearly midnight by the time Natalie reached Brunswick House. As she opened the door of the penthouse, she was thinking she'd be glad to get to bed. Then all thought stopped. Inside the hallway, Roderick and Isabel stood close together, her hand on his arm. For a frozen moment the three of them looked at each other. Then Natalie turned and stumbled outside. The lift she'd just stepped out of was still waiting with its door open and like a homing pigeon she went into it, the doors gliding shut as Roderick reached the door of the flat. She heard him call her name as the lift started its descent.

As soon as its doors opened, she ran across the marble hallway and down the steps. One of the other residents was stepping out of a taxi and, acting purely on instinct, Natalie climbed inside and gave the address in Tavistock Mews. The girls wouldn't have been in long. She hadn't her key with her, so rang the bell, hearing the chain go on before the door opened a crack, then Jill's startled voice. 'Natalie! Whatever's happened?' She fumbled with the chain and the door swung open.

Natalie said tautly, 'Roderick has one of his women at the flat. Could I spend the night here?'

Polly had emerged from the bathroom, toothbrush in hand. 'But she isn't staying, surely?'

'No, she was probably just leaving. But he gave me his word—' She paused to draw enough breath to continue. 'He gave me his word not to see her at the penthouse.'

'But if you were out—'

'That's not the point. It's my *home*. I won't have her there!'

Jill and Polly exchanged a glance. Then Polly took Natalie's arm. 'Come along, honey, your bed's waiting.' The bed from which she had stumbled to answer the phone call summoning her to Scotland.

It wasn't the fact that he was seeing Isabel, Natalie assured herself, but that he was seeing her at the flat. And before she could stop herself, she wondered if they'd made love. Still, if he couldn't keep his word, it released her from hers. He could go to his father and make his confession. As Elizabeth had said, the old man would be upset, but not fatally. And tomorrow morning she'd phone the agency and re-register. Whether or not she believed in these plans they kept her thinking positively instead of indulging in an orgy of grief.

She was up at seven and they had breakfast standing in the kitchen as always, the other girls with an eye on the clock. They didn't ask her plans and she didn't volunteer any. And at eight o'clock the doorbell rang.

'Post!' said Jill, and went to answer it. They heard an exchange of voices in the hall, and Natalie turned to see Roderick in the doorway. He was pale and there were shadows under his eyes. He nodded to Polly and said quietly, 'Come along, Natalie. The car's outside.'

'I'm not going back,' she said.

'Look, love, we'll have to fly,' Polly interrupted. 'But if you want to stay, you know you're welcome.' And without a glance at Roderick she left the room, Jill at her heels. Seconds later the front door closed behind them.

Roderick said, 'If you want to leave me— and I shouldn't blame you—we'll arrange things in a civilized manner. In the meantime, I'm waiting to take you home.'

'You *promised*—'

'You didn't give me a chance to explain.'

'I played right into your hands, didn't I, going out for the evening? And when I said we'd be eating afterwards, you thought you'd more time than you had.'

'Be quiet!' His voice rang round the little room, and her eyes widened. 'I'm under no obligation to account for my movements, but since you're determined to think the worst, I shall. As it happened I was—I didn't feel like staying in last night, so I went to Bob Lindsay's for a drink. I was later than I intended and only reached home minutes before you did. Isabel was waiting outside. She'd been there some time.'

Her breath was hurting her. 'You'd no need to let her in.'

'As it happened I wanted to speak to her, and it was not something we could discuss in the corridor.'

'I bet it wasn't.'

His mouth tightened but otherwise he ignored her. 'I give you my word that we hadn't moved from the spot where you saw us.'

'And after I left?'

'Isabel was right behind you. I spent the night in splendid isolation, if it's any concern of yours.'

'I don't care what you do, as long it's not in my home.'

'I see. I'll bear that in mind.'

For a second longer they stared at each other. Then he moved forward and took her arm. Stiffly she resisted. 'Natalie, I'm trying to keep my temper. How do you think I felt, with my wife rushing off into the night? I looked such a fool.'

'Ah!'

'No,' he said tiredly, 'that wasn't my main concern, though I don't expect you to believe it. But as I said, Isabel was at the flat ten minutes at most, and only because it was unavoidable. Now will you come home?'

'All right,' she said dully.

They drove back in silence but as they garaged the car behind Brunswick House, Roderick asked abruptly, 'Did you think I'd been to bed with her?'

Natalie tensed. 'I'm not sure what I thought. It was such a shock seeing her.'

'I appreciate that, but couldn't you have given me the benefit of the doubt?'

She said carefully, 'I don't expect you to change your life-style for me.'

'My life-style?'

'Well, I know you're used to—being with women—' A glance at his frozen face brought her to a halt. Without a word he got out of the car and locked it. Then he took her arm and walked her quickly out of the garage and into the building.

'I think,' he said as they went into the flat, 'that it's time we sorted a few things out.' He pushed her ahead of him into the sitting-room. 'For some reason you seem to regard me as a professional Casanova. In fact, there have only been three or four women in the last fifteen years—not excessive, would you say? And though I regard the word love as a euphemism, I've never slept with a woman I wasn't fond of. Which brings me to another point. You'll be surprised to hear I do have morals, and despite what Isabel hinted that time, I haven't been with her since our marriage.'

He drew a deep breath. 'Now perhaps we

can turn to more immediate matters. What do you want to do?' She stared at him numbly and he continued, 'We can't go on as we are, I'm sure you won't argue with that. I can't concentrate on my work or anything else, and you're clearly unhappy. If you want to go back to your friends, I shan't try to stop you.'

There was a long silence. Then Natalie asked shakily, 'Would you rather I did?'

'As it happens, no, but the decision is yours. Do you want to go?'

'Not really.'

He had to bend forward to catch the words. 'Well, something will have to change if we're to patch things up. Apart from anything else we can't keep stalling about Scotland and the fact is that if we go, there's no way we can avoid sharing a room except by telling the truth. We might as well save ourselves the trouble by owning up now.' He paused. 'And that's at the root of it, isn't it? What happened the other night? Be honest, Natalie. You owe me that.'

'It wasn't the love-making,' she said in a low voice. 'It was what happened afterwards.'

'But I apologized, and I've gone out of my way to—'

'I don't want *apologies*!' She looked up at him, willing him to understand. 'I'd expected you still to be there in the morning. When you weren't, it suddenly all seemed so—'

He stood unmoving, his eyes on her averted face. She swallowed and tried again. 'And it

160

wasn't only that you left me as soon as—it was over. You've been so distant ever since, I just thought that you—' She stopped, then finished in a rush—'that it couldn't have been as good as you expected.'

He said tonelessly, 'Oh, my God,' sat down beside her and took her hand. 'Natalie, I'm a bungling fool. I'd no idea how much I was hurting you. I was so sure it happened because I over-reacted about the Award, and that you'd regret it in the morning and blame me as much as I blamed myself.' His fingers tightened round hers. 'As for keeping my distance, that was for my own protection as much as yours. Since that night, there hasn't been an hour when I haven't wanted to make love to you.' He tipped her head back till he could see her eyes, and drew in his breath. 'Have I been completely misjudging the situation?'

She nodded, and her bones seemed to dissolve as his arms came round her with an urgency he made no attempt to conceal. 'Perhaps,' he said a few moments later, 'we should waste no more time in putting matters right.'

This time they went to his room, and when the love-making was over, fell asleep in each other's arms. It was lunchtime before they came properly awake. Natalie stirred first and lay, warm and relaxed, watching Roderick's sleeping face. Soon afterwards he opened his eyes and smiled, tracing her lips with one finger.

'What are you thinking?' he asked softly.

She looked away, frightened that her eyes might have betrayed her. 'That you were right, as long as we're together we might as well enjoy ourselves.'

The smile left his eyes. Then he said, 'Exactly! Think how much time we've wasted! Still, we know where we are now, and at least there's nothing to stop us going to Eagle's Crag.'

Later that afternoon, Polly phoned. 'Are you all right?' she asked anxiously. 'I'm sorry about deserting you, but it seemed the most diplomatic thing to do.'

'Everything's fine, thanks, Poll. It wasn't what I thought.'

'That's a relief. You mentioned going to Scotland?'

'Yes, in about ten days. I'll phone you when we get back.' By then she'd know more about Dougal McLaren's health. She wondered dully which would grieve her more, his death or the end of her marriage.

For the moment, though, she and Roderick had adjusted to their new relationship. At his suggestion, she moved her things into his room and it was hard to believe the arrangement wasn't permanent. But tender and considerate though he was, even at the height of passion he never mentioned love. Natalie concluded he was abiding by his own rules—affection and enjoyment for as long as it lasted. Closing her mind to might-have-beens, she tried to be thankful for what she had.

Meanwhile their departure for Scotland was drawing nearer. 'How long shall we be away?' Natalie asked, watching Roderick sort out his golf clubs.

'Two or three weeks. Father likes to be out of Edinburgh during Festival. I can't think why. I enjoy the atmosphere myself, and there's so much to see.'

'Will Aunt Elizabeth come to Sutherland?'

'Certainly, she never misses.'

'Then she'll realize what's happened.'

'True, and it'll be another black mark against me.'

Especially, thought Natalie, since she was aware of facts that Roderick himself was not.

Jack Drummond again met them at the airport. 'Good to see you back,' he greeted them warmly.

'How's Father, Jack?'

'In fine fettle, Mr Roddy. Impatient now to be off to the Highlands. The first blare of music from the Tattoo and he's packing his bags!'

'I hope he's not expecting us to drive up tomorrow,' Roderick commented. 'We'd like to see at least something while we're here.'

But Dougal McLaren's impatience was evident. 'Foreigners everywhere!' he grumbled. 'The place won't come to its senses till mid-September, and the sooner I'm away

163

out of it, the better I'll be pleased.'

Later, Natalie asked Roderick why his father didn't leave before the Festival began.

'The house hasn't been free till now. It's rented for a fortnight from the twelfth, for the shooting.' And, seeing her bewilderment, he explained: 'We have grouse moors and rent them out every year. The Glorious Twelfth is the start of it, and the same people have the lease every year. They won't be leaving till tomorrow, and if Father has his way, there'll barely be time to change the sheets before we arrive.'

Nor would the old man be swayed from leaving the next day.

'It doesn't matter,' Natalie said quickly, when Roderick tried to secure her a day's grace. 'I couldn't see all I wanted in one day, it would only whet my appetite!'

'Next year,' Dougal conceded, 'you can stay here and Jack'll drive me up, but I want you with me just now. I've set my heart on showing you the estate.'

'Of course,' she assured him, 'I'm looking forward to it.' And, having won his way, he smiled and patted her hand. His son was very like him, she thought ruefully.

'There was a time I feared I'd not see it again,' the old man went on. 'I'll be buried up there, when my time comes.'

'Which won't be for a while yet, from the look of you!' commented Roderick dryly.

Dougal grunted and turned back to Natalie. 'It's a grand place we have up there—moors and deer forests, fishing in the lochs, and clean fresh air to fill your lungs. Aye, it's a man's life, right enough. How that boy can prefer plittering away his time in London, I'll never understand.'

Natalie felt rather than saw Roderick tense. 'It's hardly "plittering", Father,' she said carefully. 'He works very hard and he's highly thought of, you know. His books—'

'Och, anyone can write stories, if he's the mind!' Scorn laced the old man's voice. 'But tell me how many can stalk a deer and bag a bird with a shot from the shoulder? That's man's work!'

'You're not being fair!' Natalie burst out hotly. 'Writing's as much a man's work as—as killing defenceless birds and animals! And Roderick's among the topmost writers in the country. His last book was on the short list for the Radbrook Award, and not many people can claim that! Everyone respects him except you—and the tragedy is that your opinion means more to him than all the rest put together!'

She broke off, seeing the old man's startled surprise, aware of Roderick motionless behind her.

There was a brief pause, then Dougal remarked, 'She's plenty of spirit, this lassie of yours, and I like her loyalty.' He flicked a

165

glance at his son's wooden face. 'I'd not realized you took my blethering so seriously, boy. I've a sharp tongue, but that doesn't mean I'm not proud of you.' His mouth twitched in a smile. 'It does me good to see you on television, telling those southerners a thing or two, and you write grand stories, forbye. I've read them many times.'

Roderick said slowly, 'You mean that?'

'Indeed I do, I never dreamed you doubted it. I'm not one to speak freely of things that matter, but that's not to say I don't feel them.' He blew his nose. 'Grown men, and it takes a wee lassie to straighten us out. We're in her debt, seemingly.'

Later, when the old man had retired to bed, Roderick and Natalie strolled into town to see what was happening. It was a warm evening and the streets were crowded. The buildings on the far side of Princes Street were floodlit, their shining stonework golden against the deepening sky. On the steps of the National Gallery a couple of boys were strumming guitars and several people sat below them, listening. Further down the street a crowd was laughing at the antics of a clown as he turned cartwheels on the pavement. The whole city was *en fête*, its normal sobriety forgotten as the magic of the Festival took hold.

'It's fantastic!' Natalie exclaimed. 'I wish we had longer to look round!'

'There's always next year,' Roderick replied.

'If we're no longer together, get Clive to bring you.'

She turned away, her happiness fading, and the edge was still in his voice as he went on, 'I haven't thanked you for springing to my defence earlier.'

'I'm sorry if it embarrassed you. I hadn't meant to interfere, but—'

'You never take me at face value, do you, Natalie? I said I was grateful.'

'But you didn't sound it.'

'Only because it adds still more to what I owe you. Father said we're in your debt, but he's no idea how much.'

'I don't regard it as a debt,' she answered quietly.

'How do you regard it? Our marriage, I mean. As a business deal?'

'That's what you called it.'

'I didn't know then how long it would last. I'm disrupting your life indefinitely, which I certainly hadn't intended.'

On the Castle Esplanade the Tattoo was about to begin, and the strains of the pipes drifted down the hill towards them, plaintive and haunting.

'Would you have agreed,' Roderick persisted, 'if you'd known how much would be involved?'

'I don't know.' It was hard to think back, but he'd attracted her from the start. Yes, she would probably still have married him. 'Would

167

you have asked me, if *you'd* known?' she countered.

'Well, you haven't given me an easy ride. Some of your criticisms called for a lot of hard thinking, and not only about my books. Still—' he smiled into her anxious face— 'there have been compensations I shouldn't like to have missed! Talking of which, it's time we went home. Thank God I shan't be confined to that chair tonight. It nearly marked me for life!'

And with potentially searching questions safely side-stepped, they returned to Ravelstone Place.

CHAPTER TWELVE

The long drive north was tiring and Natalie, sated with the magnificent scenery through which they had passed, was as thankful as Dougal when it neared its end. They had been climbing steadily for some time, and now started a descent towards a narrow loch with a cluster of houses at one end.

'Almost there!' he announced, his voice ringing with excitement. 'That's Strath Lennoch below. Eagle's Crag's over the next rise.'

The entrance to the estate was impressive, with a lodge at the gate and high fences all round to keep in the deer. A small boy was looking out for them and swung the gate open as the Range Rover came into sight. As the car turned into the drive, a man came hurrying from the lodge.

'Jamie Begg, the factor, Natalie,' Roderick told her and wound down his window. After the initial greetings, old Dougal leaned across.

'Did the Hardys have a good shoot, man?'

'Aye, sir, they bagged a fair number. It's all entered up for you to see when you've the time.'

'You'll be up at the house tomorrow?'

'Nine o'clock as usual, sir.' He stepped back, holding on to his son, and the car moved forward up the steep drive.

Mr and Mrs Anderson were waiting to greet them. They were the northern counterparts of the Drummonds, the wife cook-housekeeper, the husband handyman, driver and gardener.

'We recruit local staff if we're entertaining,' Elizabeth explained. 'or if there are big shooting parties. Otherwise, we manage very well.' She stopped speaking as Anderson carried Natalie and Roderick's luggage upstairs to the main bedroom and, avoiding her eyes, Natalie followed him. The view from the windows was magnificent. A formal garden surrounded the house and beyond it the forest encircled them on three sides. As its name implied, the house was built on the slope of a hill and behind it the bare rock rose stark and impressive.

'We have several eyries up there,' Roderick said, joining her at the window. His fingers touched the pendant she wore. 'Your golden eagle has come home to roost! Welcome to the family seat, Mrs McLaren.'

During the days that followed, Natalie fell into the new routine. Every morning Roderick and his father spent an hour or so with the factor, after which they would either drive round the estate in the Range Rover or play a round of golf. Occasionally after lunch Roderick drove Natalie and Elizabeth to Brora or nearby Dunrobin Castle, one of the oldest houses in Scotland, but most of his time was spent with his father, and while their new closeness delighted her, Natalie missed his constant companionship to which she'd been used in London. Only at night, in the great old bed, were they alone together, and though their love-making continued, even that was subtly altered. The closeness which had seemed on the point of developing between them appeared to have vanished in the Scottish mists.

Much of Natalie's time was perforce spent with Elizabeth, and she was grateful that, though her manner towards Roderick was slightly cool, the older woman made no reference to the shared bedroom. No doubt she had expected such a development.

During the first week, several visitors called at the house, neighbouring families who had known the McLarens for years. One such visit gave rise to an awkward moment for Natalie.

'So, Eagle, your boy has succumbed at last!' boomed Fergus Robertson, closing his enormous hand round Natalie's. 'And I can see why! She's a bonny one right enough. Even more important, the future of Eagle's Crag is ensured for another generation.'

Natalie flushed and smiled, but she was aware of her father-in-law's keen-eyed scrutiny, and when Mr Robertson left and they were momentarily alone, he said suddenly, 'You are happy, child?'

'Of course,' she answered quickly, wondering if she spoke the truth.

'There's something, some reserve between the two of you I can't put my finger on.' His voice sharpened. 'You are fond of Roderick, Natalie?'

She met his eye steadily. 'Yes, Father. I love him very much.'

'Aye. Well, that's fine. An old man's imaginings, no doubt.' He stood up, patting his pockets in search of his tobacco pouch. 'Now Fergus has seen you, everyone will want to. The invitations will start coming in, mark my words.'

He was right. A few days later they were asked to the neighbouring estate of Inverlennoch for a 'Ceilidh'. 'Pronounced "Cayley"!' Elizabeth said, laughing at Natalie's expression as she read the card. 'Traditionally song and dance, but knowing

171

Ross McIntyre it'll be a bit grander than that. The whole neighbourhood will be there and you'll be the star attraction, my dear!'

Roderick said nothing, and his aunt's eyes followed him thoughtfully as he walked out of the room.

Inverlennoch was a larger estate than Eagle's Crag and the house more opulent. That evening it was full of people and Natalie was grateful for Roderick's presence at her side as introductions were made—far too many for her to link names and faces. Afterwards, her memory of the evening was a confused blur of Scottish dancing, tunes on the pipes, and a sumptuous buffet of salmon and rare beef, Athol Brose, flawns and honey cakes. It ended with a fiddler from the village playing a selection of old Scottish tunes, rousing choruses in which they all joined giving way to laments and lovesongs, *Loch Lomond* and *Will ye no' come back again?* Probably not, thought Natalie achingly. '*Better loved ye canna be*', they sang, and across the room she encountered Roderick's steady gaze.

The selection finished traditionally with *Auld Lang Syne* and as everyone scrambled to their feet Natalie lost sight of Roderick. Her hands were seized by men whose names she couldn't remember, and she wanted to cry.

That night she was asleep before Roderick came to bed, and the next day he was off at first light with Jamie Begg. Miserably, Natalie guessed what he was feeling. These were the people among whom he'd grown up, lifelong friends whom he resented having to deceive over the circumstances of his marriage. Yet with Dougal McLaren so much improved in health, there seemed to be no solution.

But there she was wrong. After supper a couple of days later, Roderick said, 'Come for a walk, Natalie.'

A glance at his set face did nothing to reassure her, but she changed her shoes, slung a wollen jacket over her shoulder, and joined him on the drive where he was waiting. Something about his manner reminded her of the time he had taken her to Queen's Park. On that occasion he had unemotionally proposed their marriage. Perhaps now, equally dispassionately, he'd propose to end it.

They walked in silence alongside the trout stream where midges hovered in the evening air, over the stone bridge and on to the springy turf at the foot of the mountain. Once, she stumbled on the uneven ground, but he made no attempt to help her, nor to take her hand. They climbed steadily without speaking until, unable to bear the suspense any longer, Natalie said jerkily, 'What is it, Roderick?'

The sound of her voice seemed to surprise him, as though he'd forgotten she was with him. He stopped, resting his hand against a stunted tree and staring out over the roof of Eagle's Crag to the sheet of water beyond.

Again she was struck by a sense of *déjà vu*. Perhaps there was more of the Highlands in his blood than he realized, since in moments of crisis he instinctively made for the highest point of land available. His voice shocked her back to the present.

'I'll have to tell him, Natalie.'

Not yet! Oh, please not yet! she cried silently, but aloud she murmured, 'That's up to you. It always has been.'

'I can't go on deceiving him, now that we're so much closer. It's the only barrier left between us. God knows how he'll react.'

'He's stronger now. He can take it.'

Roderick turned to her, his eyes dark and unfathomable. 'I don't think you realize what I'm saying. The—arrangement between us is at an end. There's nothing to keep you here any longer.'

Down by the loch a skein of geese flew in formation to their night-time roosting. In the distance a plume of smoke rose from some crofter's fire. Natalie's voice sounded equally far away. 'Are you asking me to go?'

'Yes.' The single word was brutal, uncompromising, and she flinched. He went on flatly, 'Since it was all for Father's benefit, it'd be pointless to keep it up once he knows the truth.'

She moistened her lips, asked with almost academic interest, 'And you won't be needing me as a secretary?'

'It wouldn't be feasible, would it, after all that's happened? Better to make a clean break.'

'Just as you wish.'

'Joe will drive you to Inverness and you can fly to London from there. You have a key so you can collect your things from Brunswick House. Incidentally, I've arranged for an annuity. A single payment didn't—'

'When do you want me to go?'

'I suggest first thing in the morning. No point in long-drawn-out farewells.'

'But I can say goodbye to your father and aunt?'

A nerve jerked at the corner of his mouth. 'It would be better not. I can explain.'

'You expect me to leave without a word, after—?'

She choked to a halt, feeling her control slip at last.

He said harshly, 'I'm trying to spare you as much as possible. For God's sake, Natalie, you knew this would happen sometime. Surely the important thing is that you're free?'

'But I don't like being so—dispensable.'

'*Dispensable?* My God, if only you were! It's because you're the exact opposite that we're in this position now.'

She stared at him whitely and he wiped a hand across his face. 'I'd hoped to avoid all this, but I suppose you've a right to know. I've discovered that I love you, Natalie. How's that for poetic justice?'

175

Her eyes closed, reopened, but she made no sound.

'It's a development I hadn't even contemplated. God knows when it started, but I didn't realize until we made love the first time. You were right; I'd never "made love" before in my life, and the difference was— indescribable. Which is why I panicked.' He paused, and added reflectively, 'I almost told you once, but you made some flip remark and I stopped in time.'

'Roderick—'

'Isabel saw how things were going. Or so she claimed that last night, when I ended our association.' He stared out across the darkening valley. 'You asked me the other evening if I'd have married you, had I known how it would be. The answer has to be no. I was quite content before, in control of myself and everything else. Now I know what I'm capable of feeling, it will never be the same.'

Natalie said wonderingly, 'You've no idea how I feel, have you?'

He moved impatiently. 'Embarrassed, I imagine. I'm sorry. I hadn't intended to burden you with this.'

'I mean, how I feel about you.'

'I've a pretty good idea, so don't try to sugar the pill.'

'I shan't. I think you're arrogant and stubborn and much too used to getting your own way.' He was staring at her through the thickening air, and the expression on his face constricted her heart. 'And,' she added softly, 'I love you with every bone in my body.'

There was a long silence. Then he said jerkily, '*What* did you say?'

'That I love you. Ask Aunt Elizabeth if you don't believe me. I told her in London.'

He said, 'But I've been bracing myself for days to—' He moved towards her, gripping her shoulders and staring into her face.

'I know how you feel,' she told him unsteadily. 'I can hardly believe you love me, either.' Then, as he continued to gaze down at her, she added with a choked little laugh, 'Aren't you ever going to kiss me?'

It was dark when they returned to Eagle's Crag. The lights from the sitting-room spilled onto the drive in a golden pool. Inside, they could see Dougal by the newly lit fire, Elizabeth at his side.

Roderick's hand tightened on Natalie's. 'Ready, my darling?'

She nodded and they went inside. The other two turned questioningly as they stood just inside the doorway. Roderick said quietly, 'Father, we—or rather, I—have a confession to make.'

Elizabeth made a sudden movement, then remained still as, carefully choosing his words, Roderick told them the truth about his marriage. When he finished speaking there was silence. Dougal McLaren was gazing into the fire, his gnarled hand clenched on the arm of his chair. Roderick added placatingly, 'We did deceive you, Father, but from the best of motives.'

'And I complicated matters by staying alive.' The old man looked up, his eyes moving from their apprehensive faces to their tightly linked hands. 'And what now?'

'If you'd asked this morning you'd have had a different answer, but we've just discovered that we love each other.'

'Thank God,' Dougal said quietly.

Elizabeth ran forward, her eyes full of tears. 'Oh, my dears—it's what I've been praying for!'

Roderick was still watching his father's face.

'Are you waiting for my blessing?' the old man challenged him. 'You had that two months ago.'

'Your forgiveness, then.'

His father raised an eyebrow and smiled slightly. 'Very well, my boy, I forgive you—for two of the happiest months of my life, and for choosing Natalie.'

Roderick smiled broadly. 'Actually, Father, it was you who chose her, and I'll be grateful for the rest of my life!' And he went forward to take his father's outstretched hand.